Project Chick II

What's Done
in the Dark

Project Chick II
What's Done in the Dark

Nikki Turner

 St. Martin's Griffin ✖ New York

This is a work of fiction. All of the characters, organizations, and events portrayed in this novel are either products of the author's imagination or are used fictitiously.

PROJECT CHICK II: WHAT'S DONE IN THE DARK. Copyright © 2013 by Nikki Turner. All rights reserved. Printed in the United States of America. For information, address St. Martin's Press, 175 Fifth Avenue, New York, N.Y. 10010.

www.stmartins.com

ISBN 978-1-250-00143-6 (trade paperback)
ISBN 978-1-250-02341-4 (e-book)

First Edition: March 2013

10 9 8 7 6 5 4 3 2 1

This book is dedicated to:

My sweet, little angel,
Malonia Asha Evans.

From the day you graced us with your presence,
YOU have made MY universe so much more happier!
Always know you can do ANYTHING your heart desires.
The world is yours, baby girl!

&

To every "Project" Chick
who aspires to do better!
After all we are ALL working projects.

In Loving Memory of Vaunte Carthorn,
You are truly missed!

Acknowledgments

First and foremost I have to thank God from whom all the blessings flow; without his love, favor, grace, and mercy nothing is possible.

My two children, Kennisha and Timmond, you inspire me more than you could ever understand! Seeing you both evolve into young adults, climbing toward your goals, only empowers me to keep plowing forward. Please remember in whatever you do that there is always room to grow, to learn, to love, to read, to strive, to dream, to give, to accomplish, and to be a blessing to others. The world is truly at your feet! Pick it up and run with it as only us Turners can! It goes without saying, know that Mommy is always here for you. NO MATTER WHAT! I LOVE YOU!

Marc Gerald, for being more than a literary agent. You are my true friend. Thank you for that—and for connecting the dots so that I'm able to continue to do what I have a deep passion for. My editor, Monique Patterson, for understanding and believing in my vision as well as giving me such an amazing opportunity to give my readers what they have been asking for

for so many years. My sister and homie Melody Guy, I have learned so much from you. Thank you for helping me perfect my craft over the years we worked together and always being genuinely happy for me—I would have never thought that a working relationship could bloom into such a wonderful candid friendship. Thank you!

Many thanks to my family and friends. In addition, God has truly surrounded me with some extraordinary folks who love me through it all—the bad, good, happy, and sad. I'm especially grateful to: my mother, for your undying love; my aunt Yvonne for not only always having my back, but for consoling me through it all. Craig, your unconditional love and friendship— truly you are the best. Farad, your undying support to me. My cousins: Lil Dre AKA Mr. Fix it all, for your spirit and for always wanting to help; Cousin Evan, for keeping it real. My brothers: Tim Dawg, your profound words and insight on my life; Curt Bone, for keeping me up on that good game; Tony Rahsaan, always ready to come to the rescue, when it really counts. My sisters: I'm priviledged to have you two in my life. A real class act, Bonnie Greer, for always knowing or finding the right answer, whether I want to hear it or not. You are what I always imagined a sister should be. Princess (Lopez), your spirit is super-amazing, you are truly my ride or die, and I love you and want you to have nothing less than the absolute best! Nurah, though we live worlds apart, thank you for being only a plane ride away when I need you. Andrea Chawatr, for always reminding me that I'm a superstar. I love you for being so empowering.

A trillion thanks to my loyal and faithful readers! Thank you so much for your never-ending support for anything I write. You keep the pressure on me to keep creating and because of you I strive to bring you the best stories I can conjure up. Without you, I would not be living out my dream. Eternal love and appreciation!

If I forgot to name anybody, please know I'm under deadline, so charge it to my head not my heart.

Project Chick II

What's Done
in the Dark

The Beginning, Part 1

Happy Birthday

Khalil "Lucky" Foster sauntered out of the Star Bright strip club at 4:13 A.M. alone. A treacherous drug entrepreneur, Lucky had quickly risen to the upper ranks of Richmond's underworld hierarchy. Rumors of his violent extracurricular activities infested the city like fleas on a homeless dog. There was no denying he could be called a lot of things, all mostly nefarious, but one thing was for sure: Lucky was the life of the party. He certainly knew how to have a good time, and everyone else knew it too. He had made it rain that night in the club, throwing around over ten thousand dollars, making the night of a lot of half-naked dancers.

He was slightly inebriated from the number of Henney shots that went straight to his head, somewhere in the double digits. "Twisted" would be an understatement, but in his mind he was still well aware of his surroundings, and was well enough to drive home.

"Happy Born Day," he whispered to himself with a smile.

He was only thirty-four years old and filthy fucking rich, which was no small task for a kid who grew up in the hood, barely finishing high school. Most cats from the projects were either killed or incarcerated before reaching the legal age of twenty-one. But Lucky wasn't most . . . he had taken absolutely nothing and turned it into something.

People, mostly haters, debated whether his bankroll grew because of his hustle or because of pure luck. Dudes had been calling him Lucky since he was fourteen years old, but as he got older and began grinding, Lucky started to hate that nickname; he felt like it was a jinx and mitigated his accomplishments. Lucky believed that his success and longevity in the game was a product of his fearlessness and brains—not something that happened by chance. The name Lucky was for losers and he considered himself to be nothing less than a bona fide winner. He wanted to be addressed as Khalil, but the name Lucky stuck hard in the streets, and after his heinous reputation grew he was glad that no one referred to him by his government name.

As he made his way through the parking lot, Lucky did a quick, but practiced, scan of the area. He noted that there were a couple of security guards, two hot chicks trying to get into a blue Honda, and a clown wannabe pimp, holding the girls up, trying to spit game.

Don't waste your time, playboy. Those two are way out your league, he wanted to tell the dude but, instead, he chuckled and minded his own business and kept moving.

He was only a few feet away from his own whip: a white 2002 big body–style Lexus. The Japanese luxury vehicle wasn't supposed to be available for purchase until at least another two months, but that rule only applied to regular cats. He smiled and tapped the automatic starter on the key ring. Like a kid with a new toy, he got a rush when the engine jumped to life. It purred like a wild exotic jungle cat. The car was a birthday gift to himself. *Life is good, ain't it?* he thought to himself with a wide smirk.

Khalid thumbed the keypad a second time and the door locks released. Inside, the cocaine-white leather seats molded to his body as he sat. Beanie Sigel's bootleg CD already leaked out into the streets.

"What Ya Life Like" was already pouring from the high-tech stereo.

"Life's pretty damn good," Lucky quipped as he sang along with Illadelphia's new phenomenal ode to survival.

A few minutes after pulling out of the strip club's parking lot, a car rolled up from behind, a little too close. Lucky instinctively palmed the black .40 caliber Glock that lay in the passenger seat, but then aborted the maneuver. The rearview mirror revealed a young lady trying to apply lip gloss and drive at the same time, a reckless combination.

"Beauty before safety," he said to himself as he shook his head and, for the first time that night, let his guard down. Lucky managed to see in the mirror that she didn't need any cosmetic improvements. He let her get a little closer so he could get a better look. *Goddamn this chick was gorgeous.*

He wished she had been in the club. *I definitely wouldn't be spending my born day alone.*

Lucky could tell she had noticed him checking her out because she held his stare and started seducing him with her eyes. When she saw she had his undivided attention, she took full advantage of it. She smiled and blew him a kiss.

Oh, no, she didn't.

Then she followed up with a sexy tongue wave.

Yes, she did.

When the light turned green, she sped past him in her convertible Mercedes.

Fuck it. It's my birthday, after all. If God wants to send me an angel, who am I to turn down his gift?

Lucky pressed the gas pedal, careful not to drive over the speed limit as he kept one eye on the road and the other on the girl with the hypnotic lips and dimpled cheeks. She made it easy for him to catch up. When he did, she was on the phone, but her eyes were on him.

She watched him watch her lips move. Then she winked.

Lucky smiled and returned the gesture.

For a moment he thought he might have recognized her from somewhere but immediately dismissed the notion. He never forgot a face, especially one as pretty as hers. She now let him take the lead, and she followed. He loved a woman who knew how to fall back and let a man be a man. The angel was now following him, waiting for Lucky to make the next move. By the enticing look in her eyes, he knew there was no doubt the ball was in his court and he had no intention of missing this slam-dunk.

He was contemplating the next move when he felt a jolt. The front of the chick's car had crashed into the rear bumper of his brand-new Lexus. *Women drivers.* A sheepish grin cracked her face when Lucky got out of the car to check the damage. He was sure it couldn't be much; the accident was more like a love tap than a serious automobile collision. His closer inspection revealed a broken left-side brake light and a smudge of green paint from her convertible.

Not too bad.

The price of getting his car fixed was certainly worth the

opportunity to exchange personal information with this exotic beauty.

And if her body matched her face they could swap a few other personal things.

When the door of the convertible opened a goddess with a devilish grin stepped out, giving a hell of a tongue lashing to a red Blow Pop lollipop.

Damn! This shit just keeps getting better and better. Lucky thought his eyes were in cahoots with the cognac he'd drunk and they were playing tricks on him. In fact, they had to be. Life was good indeed.

It was not only his birthday, but it was no doubt his lucky day.

She was built like a female superhero. He had watched naked women parade around on and off the stage at the strip club all night and yet none of them could hold a candle to this woman. He was mesmerized by her physique: her tits and ass sat up and out like accessories to an already fine work of art. As she worked the lollipop her eyes made eye contact with his. Lucky was so distracted by her loveliness that he didn't notice the van next to him nor did he pay attention to its door sliding open. And when he did notice, it was late—way too late.

A pair of hands grabbed him by the collar and neck in a vise grip. Before Lucky could resist the abduction in progress, his Pradas had already left the asphalt, and he was inside the van face-to-face with a .44 big chrome Desert Eagle.

"What da fuck?"

A slap with the gun knocked the words back into Lucky's mouth. His vision blurred for a couple of seconds. But even with hazy vision, he was able to make out the face of the man that hit him. The man with the gun in Lucky's face was Taj, who was not only his nemesis, but Tressa's, his baby's mother, older brother.

"Ain't this a bitch," Lucky said under his breath.

"I can't believe you fell for that shit, Lucky," Taj chastised. "Mr. Game Master himself, and you fall victim to your very own favorite ploy?"

Taj cold-cocked him again. This time harder, if that was possible.

Just because Lucky was caught with his pants down didn't mean he had to end up ass out. Lucky weighed his chances of being able to talk Taj into letting him live, and it didn't look good for the old birthday boy.

"You made me lose five hundred dollars," Taj said, shaking his head. "I bet your dumb ass wouldn't bite."

"But I knew you would," another voice chimed in.

The second voice had come from the driver's seat and made Lucky almost shit his pants.

Lucky recognized him immediately: Indie, his baby momma's boyfriend, who was supposed to be dead. Before now, Lucky had no idea that he had staged his own death and now he was back to seek revenge and then live happily ever after with Lucky's twin boys and his baby momma.

"How many lives do you have?" Lucky asked, unable to hide the disbelief and fear in his own voice. He could not believe that Indie and Taj had caught him this way.

"Enough to see to it that your bitch ass go first, that's fo' sho'," Indie said after ending the phone call he was on and placing the phone in his lap. "Oh, my sister, Reka, said it was too bad that you two didn't run into each other under different circumstances.

She thinks you're cute. But Reka always did have bad taste in men." Indie laughed.

Then it hit Lucky why the girl's face looked so familiar. It was Indie's face except much softer, sexier, and without question, more deadlier and definitely more deceptive.

Taj secured Lucky's hands behind his back with plastic flexi cuffs. They drove for more than two hours before reaching their destination: an isolated private patch of woods in North Carolina. The land belonged to a man named Secret, who was a friend of Taj's.

"Man, don't do this shit," Lucky began to plead to Taj. "Come on, man. After all the money I made you? I deserve better."

"It's not about the money, Lucky. It was never bout the money," Taj said. "You violated my trust and disrespected Tressa."

Lucky ignored Taj's words, even though he knew they were true, and continued to beg. "I got over five million dollars saved up. It's yours if you let me go."

"I would love to accommodate you, Lucky, but old Secret here"—Taj patted the older, straggly looking fella on the back—"really outdid himself. He done already dug an eight-feet-deep hole big enough to hold the handmade casket he built." Taj looked Lucky in the eyes. "Especially for you."

Lucky looked around and finally realized what Taj really had in store for him. And it had him scared shitless because he was claustrophobic, and his chest tightened as he began to beg. "If you going to kill me, just go ahead and shoot me, but man, don't put me in that damn hole alive." If he had to die, he wanted to die like a man, a gangster, with real gunplay, not suffocate to death underground in pine box. In his eyes that was going out like a coward.

Taj had no plans to let Lucky off the hook that easy.

"A bullet would be too simple," Taj said with a cynical smile.

Taj punched Lucky in the face with all his might. "That's for Wiggles and my unborn child." He hog spit on Lucky. "How could yo' bitch ass kill a woman and a child? Especially after you know how I felt about her. For the tears I shed over her in prison and you go and do some shit like that. You deserve what's coming to you." Taj could feel himself getting emotional, so he caught himself.

"I didn't mean to kill her," Lucky said defiantly. "The poison was meant for him." He was speaking of Indie. Lucky hated the ground that Indie walked on. "Man, it wasn't meant for her." Lucky tried to convince Taj, but it was no use. "That shit blew up in my face."

Taj acted as if he didn't hear Lucky speaking, and said, "Besides, it wouldn't be right if I didn't make your ass suffer some. The way you tormented my sister with all of your petty bullshit, it's a wonder you didn't drive the girl to the asylum. I'd be less than the man or the brother that I am if I just shot yo' ass and got it over with"—Taj snapped his finger—"just like that. Ya feel me?"

If Lucky's luck had been bad before, now it had gone to shit. Indie, Taj, and Secret took turns pummeling Lucky with a bat until he was bloody and unconscious before tossing his limp body into the wooden casket. Each had different reasons but, all in all, Lucky had fucked over somebody each of them loved. Secret was in on it because Lucky had killed his brother, Peako. For Indie, it was about reciprocity; Lucky had unsuccessfully tried to take Indie's life and now he was returning the favor.

Indie felt Lucky was the type of dude that wouldn't stop until he was dead and would definitely hurt Tressa in the process. And Taj was right, Lucky was just that type.

Taj asked, "Does anyone have a knife? I want his hands to be free when we bury 'em."

Indie pulled a six-inch jagged-edge blade from the sheath he kept concealed beneath his pants leg and cut the plastic tie from Lucky's wrists.

Taj pulled out his dick and urinated all over Lucky's face. Lucky began to choke from the hot piss splashing up his nose.

"That's right—wake up, maggot." Taj shook the head of his dick twice and tucked himself back into his pants. "You wouldn't want to sleep through your own death now, would you?"

Lucky knew he was holding a piss-poor hand, but he had to play the cards he was dealt. And he wasn't too proud to beg. "Please, Taj, don't do this."

"I asked you to *please* not fuck with my sister when I was locked up, but you chose to ignore me. You didn't give a fuck." Taj spat, feeling himself getting mad all over again. He sucked his teeth. "I almost forgot," he said, turning to Secret. "Give me the bag." And then Taj said to Lucky, "I don't give a fuck."

Secret hurried to his pick-up and came back with a burlap sack in which something appeared to be moving around inside. "This is for you." Taj turned the bag upside down over the casket and a giant rat tumbled out. "Something to keep you company."

Not only was Lucky scared of tight spaces, he was also terrified of rats. Sheer horror masked Lucky's face as Secret nailed the top of the makeshift coffin shut.

They could hear Lucky fighting with both the rodent and

his demons as the casket was lowered into the ground. It didn't take long for the three of them to refill the hole.

The ride back to Richmond had been silent until Indie spoke.

"I've never felt guilty about giving a sucka exactly what he deserved," he said. "And now is no different. But I love your sister, and I don't want to hurt her or those boys in any type of way." He was thinking of the consequences. He didn't want either of them to resent him for his actions.

Taj took a good look at Indie. While Tressa had talked about each man to the other, the two men had just met. Both of Indie's parents were 100 percent Native American and he was born in New York. He had grown up on the Indian reservation. Before now, Taj had never really been interested in getting to know a New Yorker. Taj had always thought of them as bloodsuckers who migrated to the South and tried to take over the blocks and sets that the locals had built. Even in the Virginia prisons they tried—unsuccessfully—to run shit. He didn't like them, and the only reason he made the move with the dude was because Tressa trusted him. But now that Taj had gotten to know the man, he had to admit, Indie was pretty cool, for a New Yorker.

Taj said, "Don't worry about Tressa. She loves you. And as for the twins, what they don't know won't hurt 'em."

"But, what if—"

Taj interrupted him. "There are no what-ifs. Tressa is her own woman. We'll let her decide what she wants to do. Lucky has at least eight hours worth of air in that hole." Taj paused. "If Tressa wants to save the bitch nigga, we'll call Secret and have him dig 'em up. If not, what's done is done. Okay?"

"Fair enough," Indie agreed.

Once they got back to the city, their first stop was Tressa's house. They explained the situation, leaving Lucky's fate entirely up to her.

Taj had left a blowout cell phone in the casket with Lucky that only received incoming calls. He dialed the number and handed his phone to Tressa.

"Who is this?" Lucky's voice was so weak, Tressa almost didn't recognize it.

"Looks like you got yourself boxed in," Tressa said coldly.

Indie and Taj caught each other's eye, amused by her word-play but somewhat surprised by her iciness.

To Lucky her voice probably sounded like the governor calling a condemned prisoner to grant a pardon. "Help me, Tressa! Don't let me go out like this!" Lucky begged.

"Remember," Tressa said into the phone, "I told you that you were going to need me one day when you were all boxed in?" Before he could protest, she continued. "I thought it would be a prison cell, but you have to appreciate the irony." She laughed out loud, thinking about how things sometimes worked out. Tressa wasn't normally a vindictive person, but Lucky was an evil man. He deserved everything that was coming to him.

All of the years that Lucky had spent making her life a living hell had made her emotionally dead toward him, and in a twisted way, she was happy to hear that he would be erased from her life.

"You did tell me that . . . and you were right. I'm boxed in and I do need you."

She never heard Lucky speak so humbly before. But it was too little, too late.

"You can't be talking about me," she said scornfully. "I know you don't need 'broke-ass Tressa,'" she mocked, using the same words that Lucky had tormented her with when she was forced to live in the projects and go on assistance to support their children and he thought he needed his money.

Lucky nervously laughed with Tressa. He knew that he had put her through a lot of unnecessary bullshit and that she had waited a long time to get the upper hand; now that time had come.

Lucky cried out in pain. "Damn rat just bit me again! I thought I'd killed the bastard."

Tressa could hear the rodent's claws scratching against the wooden tomb. "Man against beast. You always said you would go out fighting. May the best rat win. By this time next year you will be a one-year-old ghost. But don't worry: I'll pour a cup of cheese out for you."

"Please, Tressa, I don't deserve this!"

"You deserve worse," Tressa said. "I'm the one that didn't deserve the shit you did to me for all those years."

"I'm sorry for the way I treated you," he said desperately. "What can I say? I'm just a sick asshole. Tressa, you know I'm going crazy down here."

"Awww . . . they forgot to give you a window, huh?" she said in a singsong voice, one a mother would use for her baby. "Shame on them."

"How come you being so cold, Tressa?" Lucky had the nerve to ask.

"You know why," she charged. "It's because of you, Lucky. You made me who I am, remember? If you had shown one iota of compassion toward me when I was living in the projects, walking past crackheads and drunks, dodging bullets, barely making enough money to feed your kids, maybe I would be compelled to have pity on your sorry ass."

"So what are you gonna tell my sons? That you killed their father?"

"You don't have any sons. You were no good to them when you were alive; maybe you'll be a better father to them dead."

Lucky knew when to fold his hand, but not without popping off a few choice words of his own.

He shouted, "I made you, bitch! You ain't nothing but a cum-drinking bitch!"

"You only made me hate your tiny dick, ass," she said calmly. "The worms should be arriving shortly. If you truly are 'lucky,' they'll crawl up your ass and eat some of that evil out of you."

"Fuck you, bitch!" he spat.

"Die slow, you bitch-ass, little-dick motherfucker." Tressa ended the call. She closed her eyes with no regrets and prayed that it didn't come back to haunt her.

The Beginning, Part 2

Dead Man Talking

Four months later

The three-story, French-inspired structure on the corner of Lombardy and Jefferson was once the most illustrious entertainment venue in the city of Richmond, Virginia. Well-established musicians, actors, and artists from coast to coast all looked forward to doing their thing on the famed marquee stage. And for lesser-known artists and performers, appearing at the Resurrect was something they dreamed of.

But on a hot, summer night in its heyday, the building was fire-bombed, and according to the official police report, by suspects unknown still to this day. But like any scandalous event, chatter traveled. Some thought the fire was a malicious act of cowardice by the Ku Klux Klan. Others claimed it was the owner, who at the time was in deep debt from outstanding gambling markers and vendors and needed the insurance money to pay off his markers and rebuild elsewhere. No one really knew for sure.

One thing was for certain: the doors to the famous theater

had remained closed for more than four decades, right up until last year when a brass young real estate agent from out of state with a big ego and even bigger pockets fell in love with the charred and abandoned building on sight. The businessman told his accountant that the old-school façade reminded him of a place near where he grew up in his hometown of Chicago.

After navigating through the normal bureaucratic giant spool of red tape, the renovations went baby-ass smooth. The finished product was nothing short of spectacular and, in record-breaking time, it quickly began to live up to its celebrated reputation. After being offered many suggestions and exploring many options for the name, the owner of the club decided that it was only fitting for the name to remain as it had been etched in the stone over the awning more than half a century ago: THE RESURRECT. The name felt like a good omen.

On this particular evening the newly rejuvenated hot spot was filled dangerously close to capacity with a formally dressed crowd. The place was packed partly because of the free admission and open bar, and partly because the guest of honor of the event was none other than Khalil "Lucky" Foster.

Inside the Resurrect the guests sat patiently at the custom-made dining tables that were placed around the opulent room. On top of each marbled surface was a slender onyx vase holding a single charcoal-colored rose.

Cocktail waitresses with wide smiles and stripper bodies threaded the aisles in their high heels carrying drinks for everyone in attendance. It didn't take long for the word to spread around town that Lucky was having a party, and automatically people flocked in.

The ambiance was definitely a hustler-friendly event with

Lucky's stamp all over it: hip-hop music, beautiful women, and flowing champagne. Though the attendees were mirthfully drinking, socializing, and getting caught up on gossip, people were starting to get a little antsy.

While it was expected that Lucky would probably make some smoke-filled grand entrance, the question on everyone's lips was, "Where the hell was Lucky?"

Nobody had seen him since his birthday, which was more than four months ago. Rumors of his whereabouts flooded the streets of Richmond and surrounding counties. Was he on the run and gone deep underground? Some said he had taken a stripper chick to Tahiti and married her. Some said he went to another city, opening up shop somewhere else. Or maybe he had taken all of his illegal money and just washed his hands of the game, which was the most unlikely of all the theories. Most folks suspected that he had been somewhere doing a bid. But no one had any indication about what really happened to Lucky.

"Since Lucky went MIA," one of the partygoers said, "the streets done got dryer than a mommy's pussy."

The entire table laughed. One co-signed with a high five. "That ain't no lie, my nigga."

At another table someone said, "I heard Lucky went to Colombia or somewhere down in South America to find an even better connect to further corner the market on price and product."

"That would be a real blessing, man." It was apparent by his friend's expression that life would be better for him if that was the real conclusion.

Lucky's mother, Betty, was sitting alone near the rear of the ballroom, wearing a simple but elegant black dress. Her attention was focused on the door like she was waiting for Lucky to strut through it, but her dark, bloodshot eyes told an entirely different story. The two Xanax she'd taken earlier, the makeup, and her false smile could only hide so much. It was clear that something heavy was on the woman's mind. Her shoulders were slumped, and she looked like she was carrying the weight of the world with no place to put it down to relieve her.

Tressa knew Betty well, better than anyone else in the room. Years ago, the lady had almost been her mother-in-law, and Tressa still remained cordial with her. After all, Betty was her twin boys' grandmother. In her head, Tressa replayed the telephone conversation that she had with Betty a week ago when she invited her to come to this get-together for Lucky.

"Hello, my dear, I'm having a get-together for Lucky," she'd said.

Tressa almost fell out of the chair she was sitting in. "Oh, okay," she said, trying to keep her emotions in check before asking, "Have you talked to him?"

"Chile, it's a long, complicated story but I will share everything with you after this party is over. So promise me you will come."

Tressa respectfully tried to decline. "I don't know if he'd want me there," she said.

"Well, let me speak for him. He does. Surely you know, in spite of everything, he'd always had unconditional love for you." Betty paused for a split second then reminded Tressa, "After all, you are the mother of his children."

Tressa didn't miss the fact that Betty spoke of her only son in the past tense. "I'll come if you say so." She didn't sound convincing.

"And bring your brother and your guy friend too," Betty added.

Tressa grew even more suspicious, and asked, "Are you sure that's a good idea, Ms. Betty?"

"Yeah, people grow, people change, and certain relationships have to be accepted whether we like them or not. Please, I need you to commit to this for me."

The conversation ended with Tressa saying they would come to the party.

Betty stared across the room at the table where Tressa sat with her brother, Taj, and her fiancé, Indie. They were the only people in the room who knew for sure that Lucky wouldn't be showing up tonight or any other night.

Taj peeped his sister making eye contact with Betty. "How does she know he's dead?" Tressa said under her breath to her brother. "There has been nothing in the papers or on the news."

The invitations that were sent out by Betty had been simply inscribed:

COME CELEBRATE THE LIFE OF
KHALIL (LUCKY) FOSTER
ETERNAL BALLING

Taj leaned in closer. "She doesn't know anything," he said after taking a long swallow from his glass of cognac. "At the worst, she can only assume, but she isn't the type of woman to make assumptions." He took a quick look at Betty and then pointed to his sister's drink. "Take a sip and stay cool. Everything is everything."

Taj didn't want his sister to fall apart with everyone watching her every move. Even though Tressa never gave him all the details about the relationship between her and Lucky, Taj knew that it had been hell. After all, he knew firsthand what kind of guy Lucky was.

Back during what now seemed like an eternity ago, Taj and Lucky used to be boys. But as often happens, the best of friends became the worst of enemies.

Taj and Lucky had gotten super cool with each other about eight years ago when they were being held in the city jail awaiting the outcome of separate cases. Once Taj blew the trial, he knew it was going to be a minute before he hit the bricks again. He knew his hands were tied and was tired of seeing his sister scrambling, trying to hold it all together for him and her. Taj wanted nothing more than to take care of his sister, try to help her with her bills, and alleviate the burden of her having to take care of him while he was incarcerated. The cost of her going to college was enough, and worrying about him could be the straw that did her in. He didn't want her to stress so she could go to school and make a better life for herself. Taj was forced to make a hard business decision and a deal with Lucky. He turned Lucky onto a big-money, once-in-a-lifetime financial come-up and a top-notch cocaine plug to boot.

All Lucky had to do in return for Taj's gift was to eliminate one of Taj's antagonists, an African dope dealer that Taj no longer saw eye-to-eye with. Taj knew that once he presented the business proposal to Lucky, he would bite. After all, it was a once-in-a-lifetime opportunity for a hood dweller with a fucked-up attitude about everything life had offered thus far. A blind man would have the sense to see the potential, and so did Lucky. Without thinking twice, Lucky quickly agreed to Taj's terms.

From that point on, Lucky never looked back. In no time, he went from hood wishes to gated suburban riches. He had the best coke in Richmond, and an unlimited amount of disposable cash, which made Lucky an official force to be reckoned with in the underworld food chain.

At first, Taj was proud of his protégé and had no problems with the way that Lucky was handling business. After Lucky did the lick, he showed his appreciation by taking care of Taj's lawyer, paying him in full right off the bat. Then he made sure Taj's prison account was full so that he could afford, in abundance, the few luxuries the Virginia correctional system allowed a man in prison to have. And Taj was happy with the way that Lucky moved the work and handled their business. But Lucky made one critical mistake: Taj had made it clear from day one that his baby sister, Tressa, was off-limits. Either Lucky didn't listen or didn't care. He pursued Tressa as if his life depended on her.

To this day, for the life of him, Taj never forgot the combination of arrogance, power, and greed in Lucky's eyes the day he had the audacity to ask for his blessing to date Tressa. If Taj wasn't behind the visiting-room glass partition, he would have probably murdered Lucky right on the spot. *Fuck he thought that was?* Taj pondered the memory. *Some type of make-believe gangsta movie? Off-limits meant off-limits.*

"I wish dat nigga would walk in here," Taj whispered to Tressa with an icy glare. "I'd love to have the chance to kill 'em again."

"You can best believe she knows he's dead," Tressa said, breaking off from Betty's weary stare. "That's the reason why we're all here. I can feel it."

At that moment, the house lights were lowered, and the giant screen above the mahogany stage illuminated the room in a cinematic blue hue, launching another round of murmurs and commotion from the guests. Then the unspeakable happened: Lucky appeared on the video screen—bigger and larger than life—just the way he always liked it.

The room became so quiet, you could hear a mouse piss.

"I hope you bitches are having a motherfucking grand ole time," Lucky said from the movie screen with a sardonic smile, exposing all thirty-two of his pearly whites. He was wearing a black custom-made suit, black gators, and a freshly starched white shirt with onyx cuff links. Pinned to his lapel was a rose, identical to the ones on all of the tables.

Seeing Lucky up on the screen sent chills up Tressa's spine; her emotions caused a tiny bit of moisture to form at the corners of her eyes. The tears rolled down her cheeks, not because she was sad he was gone but because of all the horrible things he had done to her.

Years ago, Lucky started to become more and more obsessed with death. Although he acted like he was invincible, he was wise enough to know that as with every living thing—young, old, rich, poor, black, white, Hispanic, Asian, fat, or skinny—death was inevitable.

In the event of his sudden demise—if it went down that way—he made his mother promise him that she would put him away on his terms and his alone. And from that day, every year since, he would tape a video eulogy, updating it so his plan would go off just how he wanted it to.

For the first time tonight Betty's smile was genuine. This was her son's last wish, and it was she who made the wish a reality. Everything her son wanted was executed to the smallest detail. It was her last chance to make up for the times that she may not have been the best mother when he was a little boy. But that was a long time ago, and over the past few years she had done everything in her power to make it up to him. Betty had promised her son with all her heart and soul that she was going to make sure that this day happened the way he wanted.

Back on the screen Lucky was saying, "In case it hasn't been made clear to all of you yet"—his devious smile was unnerving—"if you are watching this video . . . it's because I'm no longer among the living. I've passed on, or in laymen's terms, I'm dead. It's just that simple: if you live hard, you die hard! Right now, I'm no doubt making my presence known in gangsta's paradise." He paused for a moment. The effect was haunting. He laughed. "Or at least putting together a team of hell-raisers to take the bitch over." He took a deep breath as if he was contemplating what he had said, before letting out a small chuckle. "But I won't bore you with my demonic mergers and takeovers."

Silence had the room on lockdown.

After the momentary shock subsided, everyone had something to say, but before they could voice their own opinions Lucky started talking again. The guests did as any normal person would do: they shut the fuck up to continued watching. No one wanted to miss one word of the fallen king's monologue.

Lucky continued. "Hell, one of you sons of bitches probably done it. I wouldn't be surprised. It was written long ago in the book *The Art of War:* 'Your worst enemies can become your closest ally and your closest ally may become your worst enemy.' "

Lucky took a pull from his cigar. "Yeah, despite what you dumb motherfuckers might think, a nigga like me read too."

Tressa drank from her glass of white wine and watched in disbelief. She knew firsthand that Lucky was a devious psychopath that was whacked out to the third power, but she hadn't known his flair for the dramatics went to this level, at least not in this way. But the writing had been on the wall, long before now.

Tressa's thoughts reflected back to the day she'd caught a flat tire while she was out with the twins. Ali and Hadji had not been even two years old. She didn't have a spare tire because Lucky had foolishly taken it out of the trunk. Nor did she have a cell phone to call for help, also thanks to Lucky's jealousy. The morning before, he had broken the phone into pieces because she was tending to the boys and had missed a call from him.

Tressa was fortunate enough to get offered a ride by an old friend of her brother named Peako. For as long as she lived and walked the Earth that was a moment that she would never forget. Once Peako had them in his truck, he shared that he was expecting a baby of his own. She could still remember the excitement in his eyes when he spoke of his pregnant girlfriend. But minutes later, as soon as they pulled up to the stoplight, out of nowhere, gunshots rang out.

Boom! Boom! Boom!

The bright light that had shone in the eyes of the man who had been so nice to help a damsel and her children in distress was cut off like a light switch and replaced with nothing. Blood and bits of brain spattered the windshield, upholstery, Tressa, and even the twins. She feared she and her children would be next. Then Lucky appeared, holding a ridiculously huge gun.

After killing an innocent man in cold blood, he turned the

gun on a girl that was riding with them. They had just come from a hotel together. The girl tried to run but the bullets ate up the distance faster than her feet. Two slammed into her back, dropping her like a bad habit. She didn't deserve to die like that; her only crime was creeping with the wrong fool at the wrong time.

Afterward Lucky drove Tressa and their boys home, locked her in the house, then went back out to clean up the murder scene.

Later, when Tressa got over her shock, she asked, "Lucky why in this God forsaken world would you kill that man for no reason?"

He simply responded, "Because I thought you were fucking him." Then he shrugged off what he had done. "My bad."

After that fiasco, it was clear to Tressa that Lucky was a danger to her and their boys. That was when she knew she had to get away from the maniac. She gave up everything—the money, the house, the cars—took her kids, and started over. But Lucky wouldn't leave her alone to live in peace. Nor would he help her provide for the boys. He went out of his way to treat her like she was a larceny-hearted dude in the street that had stolen money from him. He watched her scrape by with his sons while he lived lavish and hood-rich.

Though it was five years ago, Tressa still had ill feelings when she thought about the way Lucky had treated her after *he* begged her to give birth when he found out she was pregnant.

Back on the big screen Lucky removed a lighter and what looked to be another oversized cigar from the inside pocket of his suit jacket. He sparked up and took a pull. "I hope y'all didn't mind waiting for the show to begin, but ain't shit changed with yo' boy." He nodded and beamed in on the camera. "Dead or alive, I still ain't waiting on no one. And in case you didn't notice this here is one of them closed casket joints cause I ain't fittin' to have none of you chumps looking down on me." He exhaled a thick stream of bluish smoke.

It didn't go unnoticed that it was more than a closed casket ceremony; there was no casket anywhere in sight.

"I invited you here in this way because I believe for the most part, niggas always misunderstood the ole boy." He took another pull from the blunt before continuing. "I was always a 'shoot first, and ask questions later' type of guy. That was a quality I inherited from my environment, from the streets, from grime and larceny. A necessary skill to keep me alive."

"I guess that bullshit didn't work out so well, huh?" a liquored-up guest joked out loud.

A few people laughed. More probably wanted to, but it seemed sort of inappropriate, even if Lucky did deserve it.

The video went on for another twenty minutes with Lucky mostly talking about how much he loved his two only sons. According to him they meant the world to him.

Then Lucky stared back into the camera, and said, "To my baby mother and the love of my life, Tressa . . ." He gave that sardonic smile of his again.

At least a hundred eyes shifted to the table where Tressa was sitting.

"I may have treated you wrong sometimes, fucked a few bitches I probably could have done without, but make no mistake about it, you'll always, always, be my baby."

A few of the guests let out a chorus of "Awww," as if what

Lucky was saying was something sweet, but Tressa knew there wasn't nothing sweet in the shit Lucky was talking.

Then the softness of his voice and body language went out the window. "And regardless of how you may feel about me now, every time you look at our boys—Ali and Hadji—you gon' see me. Fuck that nigga you with. That there ain't gone never change!" Lucky screamed into the camera.

Tressa eyed Indie with a look that said, "Is this clown serious?"

Indie understood completely. He didn't show one ounce of disgust or insecurity because the one thing he was sure of was that his and Tressa's bond was stronger than words—or insults.

Lucky sat there for a few seconds breathing hard on the screen. Then he fixed his suit and his composure before he continued.

"To moms." He dropped his head and took a deep breath. "Over the years, I've put this guilt trip on you for doing the things that was necessary to take care of me and provide for me when I was a lil' boy. Mom, real talk, I respect you for always making sure I had what I needed. You are a God-fearing woman and I wish I would have taken the time to listen to you and wish I didn't disappoint you. You did the best you could do, with what you had. I love you for loving me unconditionally no matter how fucked up I was.

"And Taj?" The guests' eyes shifted from Tressa to her brother. Taj didn't pay much attention to all the people looking at him; instead he took a sip of his drink, not sure he really wanted to hear what Lucky had to say. "What can I say, man? You changed my life. Loved and respected you for it. I know I crossed the linc with your sister but I wouldn't change it for all the pussy and money in the world."

"And, Ace, my nigga to the bitter end." Eyes shifted to Lucky's homeboy, who put up his glass and poured some out on the floor for Lucky as he watched his friend and partner go out with a bang. Ace was enjoying every second of his five seconds of fame. "We did too much shit to even speak about. Don't stop living life to the fullest with me watching over ya. You know I'll be saving a bed for you in hell right beside me whenever you get here, man.

"In the end," Lucky said, "I'll have my ashes sprinkled over the hood . . . because from the hood I came, and in the hood I will always be."

Tressa asked her brother in the tiniest whisper, "Are you sure he's dead?"

"As a doorknob," Taj assured her. "This video shit had to be done at least a year ago. Look at his haircut."

Taj was right. Lucky had cut the dreads off last year.

"Drink up," Lucky said in the video. "This one is on me. That is until I see you bastards in hell."

His last words . . .

Before fading to black, Lucky sat in a chair and, facing the camera, finished the blunt while Scarface's words. "Never seen a man cry until I seen a man die" haunted the background. *This shit can't get any crazier,* Tressa thought.

Oh, how wrong she was.

Some guy stood up. Tressa vaguely recognized his face, and for no apparent reason, he pulled out a big gun and started shooting at the movie.

Trendrils of smoke wafted from Lucky's image where the

bullets had ripped through the screen. It seemed surreal. And, as if that wasn't bizarre enough, another fool began popping off shots in concert with the first.

The thoroughly entertained, and now frightened, guests started screaming, hiding under tables, and stampeding for the exit.

The next day, word in the street was that Lucky's friends wanted to make sure he went out in a blaze of fire . . . and did.

The hood was just funny that way.

1

Boys Will Be Boys

Seven years later

The month of July had two-pieced the city like an experienced, heavy-weight champion boxer walloping a malnourished and under-skilled wannabe combatant. The fight was over before it started. The winner, by unanimous decision, was the heat wave.

Local meteorologists had warned the masses about the extreme weather. There was going to be a heat index of 105 to 110 degrees, and feature the three Hs: hot, humid, and hazy. None of the so-called experts mentioned the fourth H:

Hellacious!

The streets were sweltering. The only people it didn't seem to slow down were the kids who were out of school for summer vacation and the low-level drug boys who were out of their mind for being caught in that heat, peddling everything from pills to crack cocaine.

The musical chimes of the ice-cream truck sounded

throughout the community; its presence alone was a relief to everyone, especially the neighborhood kids.

Ali and Hadji were sitting on their friend Tommy's porch kicking the bo-bo. When the loud melody from the ice-cream truck announced that it was near and on its way to the block, Tommy's little sister, Tommesha, ran out of the house in reckless abandon in chase of an icy treat. "Hold on a minute," Tommy said, putting the brakes on his sister. "How much money do you have?"

"Two big nickels," Tommesha proudly told him, anxious to get on her way.

"Girl, c'mere. That ain't enough to buy nothing." Tommy dug into his pocket and fished out a five-dollar bill.

He asked his friends, "One of y'all got change?"

Both twins shook their head, so Tommy handed his sister the five-dollar bill along with strict instructions: "Get one thing and bring my change back."

Tommesha clutched the money in her small hands and took off running.

Ali asked Tommy, "How old is your sister, man?"

"Five, going on twenty-five." They could tell he really loved her, even though he tried to act like she was a pain in his butt.

When Tommesha returned from the ice-cream truck with a red-and-white-and-blue Bombsicle, she was so preoccupied trying to get the wrapper off that she barely heard Tommy ask, "Where's my change?"

After he asked a second time, she went in her shorts pockets and pulled out a dollar and a nickel. "Here." She handed it to him.

"Where the rest of it?" he asked, knowing good and well that the popsicle didn't cost four dollars.

Tommesha shrugged her little shoulders. "That's all the man gave me." She had the wrapper off now, taking her first lick. It put a snaggle-toothed smile on her face.

"He on that same stuff, man," Tommy said to the twins, shaking his head. "That popsicle was only one-fifty, at most."

This wasn't the first time something like this had happened. Pop, the guy that operated the ice-cream truck, always cheated little kids—a quarter here, fifty cents there. The more Tommy thought about it, the more pissed he got. It was despicable the way Pop treated the kids, and Tommy wasn't having it. It was bad enough that Pop was cheating the other kids, but the buck stopped with his little sister.

Tommy was so mad he stomped over to the ice-cream truck to confront Pop. He went straight to the front of the line. "You can't cut," one of the kids protested.

"Wait your turn," Pop reprimanded. "I got enough for every-one."

"Fuck that," Tommy voiced his displeasure at the thief after glancing at the picture of the Bombsicle on the side of the truck and its price. "You stole two-fifty from my baby sister and you gotta give it back."

Pop held his ground. "You better get yo' lil' narrow butt away from my truck before you get yo'self in trouble, lil' boy." His tone was both threatening and patronizing. He added, "I ain't stole nothing from nobody. Now play like Michael Jackson and beat it, kid!"

Tommy had no proof of the theft other than what his sister

told him. What if she lost the money in her haste to start eating her frozen treat? Embarrassed and feeling conquered while unsure what to do next, Tommy dropped his head and walked off, biting his lip.

The twins watched, feeling like the entire situation was messed up. Tommy looked defeated but Hadji had no intentions on letting his friend go out like a punk. Ali, picking up on his brother's body language, got right on board.

"You strapped?" Hadji asked.

Ali nodded. "Yep."

"Time to teach this sucker a lesson."

They slow-walked their way to the truck. Pop paid them no mind; he was busy exchanging merchandise for money. The twins took one last look at each other, confirming what they were about to do next. They both had a hand on their guns, which were tucked in their waistbands under their shirts. A few of the kids saw the guns and either moved back or started to take cover before the twins busted off.

"Cheat this!" Hadji screamed when he whipped out a big black pistol. Ali followed suit.

Pop's eyes got big as a pair of ripe, fleshy plums, almost popping out of their sockets. "Oh, shit. Don't shoot," he begged, then tried to duck, but it was too late.

Both boys had already squeezed the trigger.

Pop was hit twice in the chest and once on the arm before dropping to the floor of the ice-cream truck. He thought he was going to die. Then he realized he was hit with BB's.

He regained his composure. "You son-a-bitches!" he screamed. "I'll kill yo' lil' asses!"

Pop was reaching under the counter for something, probably a gun, when Ace popped up.

Antonio "Ace" Davis was somewhat of a hood legend in the Richmond Redevelopment Housing Projects. In his prime some people actually referred to him as the King of Cyprus Court, in reference to the projects where he grew up and did most of his dirt. Now at age thirty-nine, with a six-year prison bit behind him, he mostly just went by Ace. Ace knew that kings ruled for a while, but most eventually fell or were overthrown. There was always someone new waiting to pick up the pieces and the crown. That's why he had ditched the king moniker: Ace planned to get cake forever . . . until the day he decided he wanted to pass his crown down.

"What you thinking bout doing, Pop?" Ace asked the question matter-of-factly. "It can't be what I think . . ."

At the sound of Ace's voice, Pop froze up like the popsicles he was peddling.

Pop was visibly shaken just by Ace's presence. "Th-the kid," Pop stammered, "shot me with a BB pistol."

"Stop crying like a bitch, man, especially when you deserved that shit."

Ace knew Pop was an opportunistic junkie who would do anything for a dollar. The only thing that kept him afloat was the old-ass ice-cream truck and scamming kids.

"Good thing it wasn't no real bullets, huh?" he said, trying to make himself feel better and convince Ace that he was over it at the same time.

"You should be thankful." Ace wiped his face with a towel and added the warning, "If you keep on with the bullshit, the next time you may not be so lucky. Those boys just so happen to be friends of mine."

Pop looked like he wanted to say more but thought better of it. "Sure, Ace. Whatever you say, man."

"Matter of fact, find another place to peddle yo shit at, cause if I catch you round here again, yo' luck gonna be ran out!" Then Ace told the twins, "Why don't y'all walk with me to the store? I wanna kick it with you about something anyway."

Once up the street Ace asked the young boys, "Hot enough out there for ya?"

"It's hot as fish grease out that piece," Hadji complained.

He only said it because he thought it was the slick thing to say. The heat really didn't bother him that much.

"It's summer time," Ali said. "It's supposed to be hot." The siblings were thirteen years old going on thirty. They had smarts, big hearts, and enough defiance to take them places.

Ace laughed at the boy's rational observation. "Did I ever tell y'all how much you remind me of your daddy?" he asked the identical siblings.

Ace and the boys' daddy, Lucky, were pretty cool back in the day. Together, they did some things that were best never to be spoken out loud. The bond Ace had had with their dad was one of the reasons he took a liking to the brothers when they first started spending weekends at their grandmother Betty's house. She lived on Twenty-ninth Street in a house directly on the other side of the projects.

The twins—especially Hadji—couldn't get enough of hearing about their father's war stories. He died when they were young. Their mother almost never talked about their father, which only made the boys more interested in him.

"Your daddy was a real live OG on these bricks," Ace said. "And that shit y'all did back there reminded me a whole lot of Lucky. Seriously, that would have been some shit he would have done." Ace smiled and shook his head knowing good and well there was no denying these boys were Lucky all over, but worse, because they came in a double dose.

They stepped into the Chinese food market that doubled as a convenience store and, in contrast to the outside, it felt like an oasis. The store may have smelled like dried fish and old cheese, but at least it was air-conditioned. Ace pulled the sweat-drenched T-shirt from his chest to cool off, only to watch in dismay as the fabric snapped back to its original sticky position once released.

"Get what ya'll want to drink," he said. "Or whatever else you want."

They were all looking in the big cooler where the beer and cold drinks were kept when Ace noticed the reflection of a white man coming into the store in the convex mirror that the store used to watch thieves. The caucasian dude was wearing old jeans and work boots and looked like he was on break from a construction job, except these was no construction work underway in the area. He stuck out like roaches in a box of cereal. Sometimes whites came through the projects to score drugs but never by themselves if they didn't know anyone. Besides, Ace observed, dude was too healthy looking to be chasing narcotics. Which meant, fifty bucks to a doughnut, dude was the po-po.

Ace wasn't "dirty" at the moment, but the back of his SUV was filthy enough to put him away for this lifetime and the next, if the police found it. He was glad that he'd left his truck down the block and walked to the projects when he saw the boys. Ace eased the keys out the front pocket of his pants and passed them to Hadji. "Hold on to these," he said. "And don't give 'em to nobody, ya dig?"

Hadji looked him straight in the eyes. "I gotcha, Ace." He nodded, pleased that Ace trusted him with his keys and to have his back.

"You can count on us," Ali seconded.

The cop walked up a few moments too late, missing the handoff. "Let me see some ID, Mr. Davis."

"If you already know my name," Ace asked, "what in the fuck you need my license for? I got zero time for games today." Then he added, "It's too hot for that shit."

The cop smiled like he'd heard it all before. "You're going to have plenty of time for games in prison when I get done burning your ass." He glanced at Ace's ID. "Now come the fuck with me."

"Ain't done shit to be going with yo' ass nowhere. How bout I call my lawyer first?" Ace threatened, well aware of his rights.

The twins watched the whole thing go down blow-by-blow. Ali processed every word of the exchange while Hadji looked like he was ready to kick the dude in the walnuts and help Ace rumble with the police, right then and there in the middle of the store.

Ace slid them a quick furtive nod on the sly that said, "why the hell y'all still standing here?" Not one to miss much going on around him, Ali caught on. He disappeared up the aisle, leaving his brother behind to continue and watch, but it didn't take long before Hadji had reluctantly caught up with his brother.

The cop handcuffed and then perp-walked Ace to the front door. When they all stepped back outside, the sun wasn't the only thing lightening up the block. Just that quick there were blue strobe lights from unmarked cars break dancing off the ground and buildings.

Alcohol, Tobacco, and Firearms. A.T.F.

The Feds had received extra money in their budget and decided to go back into old murder cases in the city of Richmond and surrounding counties to see what they could stir up. Unfortunately for Ace, his name was one of the first on the list of suspects. But the police were wasting their time investigating Ace for old activities. There wasn't anyone alive that could put him with a body. Ace smiled as he faced the entire neighborhood watching him being escorted out of the store and into one of the unmarked police vehicles. He smiled because he knew they wouldn't be able to hold him for long, not for anything old anyway.

The keys to Ace's Escalade felt like a brick in Hadji's pocket. Everything had happened so fast. He asked Ali, "What should we do?"

The two looked exactly alike. Both had smooth chocolate skin, long eyelashes, and jet-black hair with deep waves. Everything about them was the same down to their matching denim shorts and the purple-and-black Kobe low-top sneakers they wore on their feet.

"Do about what?" Ali shot back, already knowing the answer. He could almost read his brother's thoughts.

"You know." Hadji nodded toward the shiny black-and-chrome Cadillac truck. It was parked six blocks away from the store where Ace had been arrested.

Ali suggested, "Leave it where it is and hold on to the keys until we hear from Ace. That's the safest thing to do."

They both assumed that the truck was dirty. Ace wouldn't have given them the keys with the strict instructions, "Don't give 'em to nobody," if there wasn't something illegal inside.

"I think we should move it," Hadji countered. "Somebody probably ratted Ace out. And what if those same people called in about the truck and the po-po find drugs inside?"

For a moment, Ali thought about the scenario his twin proposed. Hadji could very well be right, but on the other hand, neither of them had ever driven a car before.

"What if we get pulled over? Or worse, what if we get into an accident and the po-po find drugs and guns inside?" Ali probed.

"You scared?" Hadji baited his twin, knowing it would do the trick.

And it did.

"Who's driving?" Ali asked.

Hadji's face sparkled with satisfaction as he held the key up in victory. "I guess I am." Then he chirped the locks. "Get in, bro."

Ali watched his brother run around to the driver's side of the car and felt that Hadji was a little bit too eager. He always was the more compulsive of the two: act first and deal with the consequences later. Ali usually thought twice before acting.

"What you think Momma gonna say if she find out?" Ali asked his brother out of the blue, stopping before he could open the door. Before it was too late.

They both feared the life out of their momma, mainly because she was so unpredictable. Tressa wore a perfect poker face all the time and they never knew quite where she was coming from or how'd she react to some of the mischievous, callous things they did. Sometimes she was overly understanding and on their side, and other times she'd flip out. And she wasn't afraid to pass out a good ass whipping when she felt she needed to. So the majority of the time when she was around, the twins walked the straight and narrow. Tressa fully understood that neither of her boys were angels, but she consistently tried hard to do her best with them.

"She'd kill us," Hadji said with a straight face.

"You right." Ali crossed his fingers for good luck and then yelled over the roof before jumping into the passenger seat. "So we better not get caught."

Inside of the truck felt like an inferno and the leather seats felt like the surface of a George Foreman grill. Hadji stabbed the key into the ignition, twisted his wrist, and the eight-cylinder engine woke straight up like a genie that had just been released from its bottle. Three seconds later, arctic air blasted from the vents of the dashboard, instantly cooling off the interior. Wish number one: granted. *So far so good,* Ali thought to himself.

A police cruiser went down the street a block ahead of them. Ali's heart dropped. "Police all over this place. We gotta be smart about this," Ali said, second-guessing his earlier decision.

"I know. What do you think we should do?" Hadji asked.

Ali looked around but didn't speak, so Hadji answered his own question. "I think our best option is to go the back way, get on the highway, and take it to the house. They don't know where we live. They didn't notice us. They think we just some innocent kids."

Ali wasn't so sure. "So we just gonna park a big-ass Escalade at the house and expect Momma to just be cool wit it? Think again, bro."

"You got a better solution?" Hadji asked. "We can't go anywhere near the projects with this truck."

"Maybe," Ali suggested, "we could park it around the street from our house. You know, like where the Park and Ride is. There's always different cars out there, and people come and go so much that nobody will really notice. As long as we go back to get it when people aren't going or coming from work, we good."

"Bet." Hadji gave his brother a dap and started to drive.

"Shit," he said when he realized he missed the highway entrance.

"Man, just go up Broad some and we can get on near the Belvidere." Hadji followed his brother's instructions.

Ali was quiet, never letting his eyes leave the side-view mirror, watching his brother's back the best he could.

Hadji tried to get comfortable, adjusting the seat and the music to his liking for the ride home but before he knew it, all hell broke loose. And he had run smack dead into trouble up ahead.

2

All in a Day's Work

Tressa was in the process of grabbing her Louis bag from under her desk before rushing out the door to get some lunch when the phone rang. She sucked her teeth at the diversion because the days of getting a break at her fast-paced position were few and far between.

"Tressa, there is a woman up here asking to speak to Eli." Tracey, the receptionist, was speaking in a low tone, and Tressa could barely hear her through the phone. "I'm not getting anywhere with her. Can you come up here and try to help her out?"

"Sure, I'll be right up." *Just what I need,* Tressa thought. *Another reason to miss lunch.* She only had forty minutes to spare before being bombarded by her boss's constant demands on her again. Nonetheless, she put down her purse and put her own personal needs aside and headed up to the reception area to see how she could be of assistance to the visitor.

As Tressa walked down the hall, she heard a woman screaming, "Somebody better give me my gotdamn money. Shit! I don't know how motherfuckers just think they can take what's mines. Fucking thieves!"

"Look, you need to tone it down," Tracey warned. "Security is on the way and will be here momentarily. I would hate it if they had to remove you from the building for your behavior."

"I don't give a flying fuck about no gotdamn security," the woman returned fire straight to Tracey's face. "Motherfuckers who doing wrong always call security to protect their asses!" She looked Tracey over and added, "Coward ass . . ."

Tracey's mug was as tight as a girdle two sizes too small, so Tressa intervened. "Tracey, there's no need for security because we are going to get this worked out." Although she was speaking to Tracey, Tressa was making eye contact with the woman who looked to be in her mid-thirties and wore a black shoulder-length bob wig.

"And who in the fuck are you?" the irate lady wanted to know, giving Tressa a once-over from head-to-toe. Then came the eye and neck rolling. "I asked to speak to the mayor, not you." Followed by teeth sucking. "You damn sure don't look like him. I know good and well yo' name ain't no Eli Walters, the lying-ass motherfucker I voted for." Before Tressa could get a word in, the woman snapped her fingers. "Humph, unless he's on some weird-ass cross-dressing shit"—another snap for confirmation—"you ain't him!" Then the woman placed her hands on her wide hips awaiting a response.

"No, I'm not Eli," Tressa confirmed. "However, my name is Tressa Shawsdale and I'm his assistant. It is my job to see how I can help the mayor help you. And you are?" Tressa asked, trying to be as civil as possible, in her best professional voice.

The woman wasn't having any of it. "You don't make no fucking decisions, so ain't a gotdamn thing you can do for me."

Tressa had to let go of a bit of her professionalism. "Look, do you want to speak, with some sense, to the person that can possibly make something happen for you, or do you want to stand here waiting to get thrown out and maybe banished from the building with the same problem that you came here with still hanging over your head? Those are your options. Because there's a difference." Tressa shot her a firm look. "You decide." After a moment of deliberation by the lady, Tressa said, "Now, let's start over. I'm Tressa Shawsdale, and you are?"

The woman seemed to be digesting the information she'd received and responded in a tone that had been turned down a few notches. "I need to speak to the head bitch in charge and if that is you then let's get down to business. And by the way, my name is Janette Jenkins." She reached out to shake Tressa's hand.

"Okay, Ms. Jenkins. Let's go in the conference room and try to resolve your issues." Tressa led the way. "But first," Tressa insisted as humbly as she knew how, "if I'm going to help you, you must lower your voice and bring the profanity to a complete halt." One of her strengths was that she was good at dealing with all types of people. She was patient but at the same time had a no-nonsense attitude, which was something Tressa had learned from years of dealing with Lucky and his random acts of bullshit. She knew how to turn a deaf ear to these kinds of attitudes and not take it personally.

Once Ms. Jenkins nodded, agreeing to the terms, Tressa lead her to the conference room and closed the door. "Now, Ms. Janette Jenkins, what seems to be the problem?" she asked as she wrote the lady's name down on top of a page in her notebook.

"Y'all motherfuckers won't give me the money that's *owed* to me," Ms. Jenkins said.

Tressa gave her the eye and then wrote down, "These folks won't give me the money that's owed to me."

"What money?" Tressa asked politely.

Ms. Jenkins looked at her like she'd asked the dumbest question in the world. "My TANF check."

"Your government-issued assistance check?" Tressa asked, wanting to be sure she had heard correctly.

"Yes, that's right. My social worker says she cut me off because I didn't fill out a paper that she sent to me. I filled it out and dropped it back off over there the same day. But she said that it was too late and I'm not getting no money. And I *need*," she stressed, "my money. I take care of my cousin's half brother's stepdaughter's baby. And that ain't cheap. Taking care of somebody else's baby ain't no fucking, I mean, ain't no joke."

Tressa listened attentively, ignoring the cuss words because she figured that they were not directed at her and that profanity was probably a part of Ms. Jenkins's everyday vocabulary. She let Ms. Jenkins go on without reminding her about the vulgarity.

"That little money they give me already ain't nothing, and now they wanna take those pennies away from me."

Tressa let Ms. Jenkins vent and get all the frustration off her chest. The strategy seemed to work, and when Ms. Jenkins observed that Tressa was listening like she really cared, her demeanor changed.

Actually, Tressa really did understand firsthand the woman's anguish; she had been in the same position, years before, waiting on her worker to hit a button. Since the office computers were still down, Tressa grabbed an enormous black City of Richmond binder and began to look for a number while Ms. Jenkins rambled on about her lazy, incompetent worker.

"Between me and you, if I ever see her in Cyprus Court I'm going to beat that bitch down like her ass stole something. For real, for real, that bitch probably really did steal my money and done brought herself one of those cheap-ass wigs she be wearing."

Tressa let her get it off her chest while she looked through the book. Once Tressa located what she was searching for, she jotted down the information.

It took all her willpower not to laugh at the way Ms. Jenkins was going in on the worker, but instead, she said, "I'm so sorry to hear about your plight. I know it's hard trying to get by on what they are giving you already and then for someone to hit a button and discontinue your benefits and not take your call . . . I know that's very frustrating."

"That's right, it sholl is," Ms. Jenkins said, happy that somebody around there was making some kind of sense.

"However, speaking to the mayor won't help you. He has no control over what's going on with your state benefits. Your situation is on a state level." Before Ms. Jenkins could crank up again, Tressa continued. "But, I have a solution for you. If you feel like your worker won't talk to you or give you an explanation as to when you are going to get your benefits, then you speak to her supervisor, which is this first number. I've written it down for you." Tressa pointed to the paper. "If they don't get you straight then call the district supervisor. And that person will get you some answers."

The woman was gazing at Tressa with a look of astonishment and appreciation when someone knocked on the conference room door.

The door opened. "Is everything okay in here, Ms. Shawsdale?" one of two security guards asked.

"Everything is just fine," Tressa assured them, punctuating it with a smile, and nodded to them. They shut the door and left.

Tressa stood up. "But you must remember, you can get more flies with honey than you can get with vinegar. So, when you call, speak to them in a calm and collected tone so you can get them to work for you."

Ms. Jenkins stood up, met Tressa's eyes, and said, "Thank you so much for everything." Then she said in a lower tone, "I didn't mean to come down here cussing and fussing, but I was just so frustrated with depending on my money and then it doesn't show up."

"Not a problem at all," Tressa said to Ms. Jenkins, who walked away at least a little happier than she was when she arrived at the mayor's office.

With that over and dealt with, Tressa rushed back to her own office to retrieve her purse. Afterward, she dashed down to the cafeteria and ordered a salad before rushing straight back to her office to gobble it down. Hopefully, she thought, the food would soothe her hunger and headache.

But as soon as she sat down at the desk, it was impossible to ignore the obscene noises coming from the back office, which was the mayor's suite.

"Oooh!" was followed by a long intense moan.

Tressa sat dumbfounded. She wanted to accuse her ears of playing a trick on her, especially when she heard the voice that followed.

"Like that?" It was definitely Eli's voice.

Whoever he was with sounded like the person really had Eli enjoying himself.

Tressa's shock quickly turned into disappointment in her boss. Did all men have to be dogs? Or was there something in the oath that said that politicians must cheat? Almost every time she turned on CNN it felt like they were reporting about a politician who was cheating on his wife, was gay, or both. Tressa had placed the mayor on a pedestal, thinking that Eli was different, but she was wrong. He was the same as the rest of the cheaters of the world.

Tressa tried to ignore them, but truth be told, she was more embarrassed. To keep from having to acknowledge the inappropriate behavior and so she wouldn't come face-to-face with the other person, Tressa decided to go downstairs to take a walk and get some fresh air. She felt so horrible that Eli was cheating on his wife. Not only because Eli had taken an oath to Ivy on their wedding day, or because Ivy was a good person, but because Ivy had been the one who actually set her up with the job. They'd met when Tressa worked part-time at Ivy's children's pediatrician's office. Ivy loved Tressa's attitude, professionalism, and her hustle so much that she asked Tressa if she wanted to make a few extra dollars by helping out Ivy with some personal projects. Being the single mother of twins with no help from their father, Tressa welcomed any kind of legitimate work that she could get. Plus, assisting and juggling tasks were second nature to her.

Tressa exceeded all of Ivy's expectations. Ivy was so impressed that when Eli began to campaign for mayor, Ivy called Tressa to come in to pitch a hand. Eli had been through numerous assistants because either he wouldn't let them into his world (making it virtually impossible for them to be productive), they could never meet his expectations, or the assistant was too young and attractive for Ivy to allow her to work for him. But Tressa was perfect, Ivy had proclaimed. Even on a part-time basis, Tressa always seemed to be one step ahead of Eli when they were campaigning, always anticipating his needs. So it was only fitting that once Eli got elected to office, he was allowed to bring in any staff he needed. Tressa was the first person on Eli's payroll after his press secretary. Haters said that she'd gotten lucky landing the job. Those riding the fence said she was at the right place at the right time. But Tressa felt it was just her doing her.

Ding.

Tressa's thoughts were interrupted by the elevator doors opening. Once she exited, she heard a familiar voice that nearly stopped her heart. "Tressa, how are you?" Ivy stepped to the side of the elevator and embraced Tressa with a hug and a kiss on the cheek.

Oh shit, Tressa thought.

Ivy was wearing a white linen pantsuit and white shoes with three-inch heels.

"I'm great," Tressa said with a bigger smile than she needed, trying to mask the guilt she felt. "How are you?"

Ivy stepped back to get a better look at her. "I was in the area and thought I'd pop in and surprise my dear Eli," she said, flipping her long, frosted hair over her shoulder. "I really like those shoes you're wearing," she added, looking down at Tressa's black-strapped Gucci sandals that went perfectly with the black pencil skirt hugging her shapely hips.

"These? I caught 'em on sale."

In spite of how much she disagreed with Eli's extracurricular activity, Tressa knew that, under no circumstances, could she allow Ivy to get on that elevator and head upstairs to the office. So with a straight face she lied. "Eli got called into an impromptu meeting." It came out more convincing than she felt. "It sounded pretty intense; it's probably going to be at least another hour before he's done. I was just on my way to lunch. How about you? Why don't you come and grab a cup of coffee, a dessert, a salad, or something with me? After all, you do have a little time to kill, since Eli has that meeting in progress."

Ivy thought about the offer while Tressa discreetly blocked the elevator like a WNBA center guarding the rim. "It's a hundred degrees outside today," Ivy said, making up her mind. "Make it a cold lemonade and you're on." Ivy held the smoked-glass lobby door open for Tressa so they could go about their business. "And," she said, "how's the wedding planning coming along?"

Tressa and Indie had been engaged for eight years. They joked that if the marriage lasted as long as the engagement they would have nothing to worry about. "Difficult and expensive," Tressa said honestly.

"They always are, no matter how small or simple you try to keep it," Ivy told her. "My motto is to do it once, do it right, and do it exactly the way you want."

When they rounded the corner Tressa said jokingly, "We have our first session of marriage counseling on Wednesday. I think he's really looking forward to that."

There was never a shortage of attractive women on Broad Street during lunch hour on a weekday, but Ivy and Tressa still hogged most of the male attention. Tressa took great care to dress conservatively, but it was impossible to conceal her shapely body and her shiny, raven hair that framed her pecan-toned face like a piece of priceless artwork hanging on the wall of the Museum of Fine Arts.

"I'm so happy for you," Ivy said sincerely. "And the offer still stands if you should need any help with the wedding planning or just need to vent about anything at all, feel free to call."

"Thank you, Ivy, but you've already done so much," Tressa said as she went into her purse, palming her BlackBerry to text Eli.

Please wrap up what you are doing. Ivy is downstairs now! I'm stalling! But don't know how long I will be able to.

Tressa hit the send button and then focused her attention back to Ivy. "I had no idea it had gotten this hot out here." The rays from the sun combined with the humidity had caused a sheen of perspiration to form on her brow. "Let's get a sandwich and something to drink from here." They were standing in front of a Greek deli a block from city hall; Tressa loved their turkey sandwiches. Hopefully, by the time they were done, Eli would be more appropriately prepared to see his wife.

Ivy spoke passionately about fund-raisers and nonprofit charities while they ate and drank lemonade. Though Tressa tried to focus on the conversation she was on pins and needles hoping that she wouldn't get caught in the middle of Eli's covert affair. *How could Eli do something like this to such an amazing woman?* The thought sort of made her wonder if Indie would ever cheat on her. She had never suspected Indie of cheating or anything remotely close, but Tressa was sure that Ivy hadn't imagined Eli cheating either. Eli fucking some bitch, in the middle of the day, on his desk.

"By the way," Ivy asked, "how are the boys?"

"Being boys," Tressa said, happy that the conversation had changed to something she didn't have to lie about. "They're over at their grandma's house right now. They spent the night."

"Those boys of yours are so adorable. And they've matured so much since I met you."

While sitting talking to Ivy, Tressa saw Rosey come in. Tressa wanted to become invisible because this wasn't the place or time that she wanted to run into Rosey. Rosey was the nosiest person in all of Richmond and always was in the mood to throw dirt with no regard of who was around. She seemed to somehow know everybody's business in the hood. Tressa often wondered why Rosey wasn't working for the police or the news, because she always had breaking news and insightful information on everybody. Tressa knew that whatever Rosey had to say to her was going to be negative.

Tressa excused herself from the table and headed to the restroom and, just like she guessed, Rosey followed her. Tressa was in front of the mirror applying lip gloss when Rosey sidled into the small, two-stall restroom.

"Hey, girl, I thought that was you," Rosey said, looking Tressa up and down while chewing a piece of gum like it was the last supper.

Tressa looked at Rosey. "Hey, how are you, Rosey?"

"Everything is everything," she said. "You looking good these days. Work and love seem to be really working for you."

This was a first, Tressa thought. Rosey actually had something good to say. "Thanks, girl." And then Tressa told a white lie, "You look nice too."

Rosey looked at herself in the mirror, as if she was saying, "Really?" "That goes without saying," she said with a smile, admiring her own self in the mirror.

Then there was an awkward silence between the two, until Rosey broke it. "Well it was good seeing you."

"A pleasure it was," Tressa said, keeping it short and sweet.

Rosey opened the door to leave. Then, as if she just thought of something, shut it. "I know the job and wedding have you busy but don't you think you should pay more attention to your sons?"

Tressa gave Rosey a look that said, "I haven't the foggiest idea what you could possibly be talking about, and bitch how dare you talk about my parenting."

While Rosey searched Tressa's face for some kind of emotion, internally Tressa was talking herself into not taking her earrings off and smacking the cowboy shit out of Rosey for insinuating that she was being less than a mother to her two prized possessions. *This bitch got balls.*

Rosey knew she was hitting below the belt so she tried to make it sound like she was only concerned. "I'm just saying, I've noticed that since your boys have been over Lucky's momma's house, they seem to be hanging around Ace a little bit too much. Like he their 'strip daddy' or something."

"Strip daddy?"

"I didn't mean nothing, but you know I don't want him to turn your sons out. Lord, it would be a shame for them boys to walk in their daddy's footsteps. You know I don't think the streets is ready for that terror again in a double dose." Rosey was shaking her head as if thinking about it was not a good thing.

Tressa was shocked to learn that the boys had been around Ace. She was about to ask more questions when Ivy walked in. The bathroom was a bit too small for the three of them, so Rosey took heed and opened the door to exit, but not before saying, "You may want to look into that."

"Uh, thanks, Rosey." Tressa tried to pay attention to Ivy, who was talking a mile a minute to her from inside the stall, but all she could think about were her sons.

She knew her boys in and out and could only hope that they were not into any mischief, but that was wishful thinking. Mischief was their middle name and if they were influenced by the wrong person, God only knows what they might get into. But she wasn't going to let a conversation with Rosey, of all people, get into her head. That didn't mean she wouldn't check into it, though.

As Ivy and Tressa strolled back to city hall, Tressa glanced over her shoulder and noticed a black Escalade speeding and swerving out of control. It was about a hundred yards away, heading in their direction. Ivy was so engrossed in conversation that she didn't see the potential danger coming. Everybody around them started to move out of the way. And before Tressa's brain could send the message to her mouth to scream or point to alert Ivy, the Escalade was less than a hundred feet away, speeding at an all-time high. All Tressa saw was danger, and Ivy was so caught up in her nonprofit talk that she didn't notice anything. It seemed like her mind was taking too long to communicate with her mouth to warn Ivy.

Fifty feet away . . .

Twenty-five feet away, and Tressa's vocal cords still weren't cooperating.

Ivy still hadn't seen the luxury gas-guzzling tank bearing down in their direction.

Fifteen feet away . . .

It looked like the out-of-control SUV was picking up speed. Instinctively, with all her strength, Tressa pushed Ivy out of the way, knocking them both to the ground. The SUV missed the two of them by only inches before taking out a parking meter and side-swiping the building. They were so close that the debris from the collision covered their clothes, and when Tressa looked up all she saw was the Escalade's brake lights backing up and taking off.

In less than fifteen seconds before Ivy and Tressa could get their composure, people surrounded them asking if they were okay. In the background, they heard sirens, letting them know help was on the way.

Ivy clutched Tressa. "You saved my life! We could have been killed."

Tressa was still in a mild shock and couldn't believe what happened herself. The EMT worker took them both to the ambulance to check their vitals. Both of the ladies were fine, besides being a little shook up. Ivy's white suit was filthy, and Tressa had broken a strap on one of her sandals.

Eli came running toward the scene. "You both need to go to the hospital." He seemed more in shock than they were.

"We're fine," Ivy said as she hugged Eli.

The EMT technician explained that they'd taken a hard fall, but under the circumstances, were okay.

"Are you sure?" he said, analyzing the situation.

"I think Tressa deserves the rest of the day off," Ivy said. "Hell, she deserves the rest of the year off, with pay. If it wasn't for her I woulda been a goner."

Eli raised his eyebrows. "She saves my life everyday in more ways than one." He let go of Ivy, took Tressa in his arms, and whispered in her ear, "Is this what you do for a diversion to save my ass?" And out loud to Tressa, he said, "Thanks for everything."

"All in a day's work."

3

The Getaway

Everybody on the street turned toward the screeching noise of the tires coming to a stop when the out-of-control SUV side-swiped the wall of the old Colonial movie theater, barely missing unsuspecting pedestrians. The onlookers were surprised by the afternoon accident and by what happened next.

"Go! Go! Go!" Ali told his brother, glad they were both wearing their seat belts. "Keep going!" *At least we did something right,* he thought. The dark tinted windows shielded them from the prying eyes of the people on the block trying to get a gander at the reckless driver behind the wheel of the Escalade.

Scared shitless, heart pounding, and palms sweaty, Hadji jerked the wheel of the Escalade, trying to get it back on the road where it belonged.

"Pull off! Pull off!" was all he could hear of Ali screaming in his ear, and it wasn't helping any. Damn right he was going to keep going. There was no other option. He smacked into two parking meters before finally getting the rubber back on the asphalt, almost knocking a man over.

Everything had been going smoothly until he took his eyes off the street (it felt like only for a split second), trying to figure out how to work the touch screen CD player. He wanted to play the new Gucci Mane CD that he found in the console.

After Hadji managed to buck off the sidewalk, Ali looked back through the smoked-glass rear window and surveyed the damage. "Oh, shit!"

Hadji heard the panic in Ali's voice, and Ali almost never panicked. "I hope I didn't fucking kill somebody," Hadji said to his brother, trying to get an update or some kind of information out of him. After Ali took too long to respond to his comment he began to worry. "What is it? Man, just tell me."

"You don't even want to know." Ali looked like he had seen a ghost.

If he had killed someone . . . shit! "Tell me," Hadji said, more impatient than he already was.

"You almost killed Momma!" Ali said, wide-eyed with a terror of emotions all over his face.

"I did what?" Hadji said, scared to death, slamming on the brakes. *Skurrddd.* The traction from the brakes made a loud noise and marked the street. He took his feet off the gas, looking for an opening in the traffic to spin the SUV around; there was no doubt he was going back to check on his momma.

"Not a good idea." Ali recognized the indecisiveness in his brother's face and though he wanted to go back too, he knew for sure that it wasn't a good idea. "She's okay," he said. "You didn't hit her. Keep going." He couldn't believe he and his brother had almost run their mother over with an SUV that was probably filled with drugs and his advice was to keep going. *What next?* he thought.

"You sure?" Hadji said, because *he* sure as hell wasn't sure. He secretly wished for a do-over, but this wasn't a video game or television show, this was real life and he had to roll with the punches.

Two blocks from the 95 North entrance, Ali said, "Yeah, I'm sure. Get on the highway before somebody gets the license plate number."

"What if they already did get the plate number?" Hadji asked his brother.

Ali's head swiveled from window to window looking for signs of the police. As they turned onto 95 he saw blue lights flashing close to where the near-catastrophic incident jumped off. As for his brother's question: those that weren't trying to save themselves from being run over were busy trying to see who was driving inside the truck. He hoped. "If that's the case then we shit out of luck," Ali said.

"But let's deal with one problem at a time."

Surprisingly, Hadji was handling the Escalade a lot better now. The accident, which could have been a lot worse, seemed to help him to focus on driving and not all the buttons on the dash. Maybe it wasn't too late?

"Do you think she seen us?" Hadji worried.

"No. I don't think so, thanks to the tinted windows."

Hadji's adrenaline was rushing a million miles a minute and Ali kept watching the mirrors. For the moment everything looked to be okay.

"How do we explain the accident to Ace?"

Silence.

"For all we went through," Ali told his brother, "he should be able to accept a little minor damage as long as his package is safe."

"Let's hope so."

4

The Trip To Grandma's

The twins made it home safely and hid the truck before Tressa got home from work. When Tressa finally did make it home she was exhausted from all the day's activities. So they ordered a pizza and watched a movie. The boys lied to Tressa, telling her they'd asked Betty to bring them home. They claimed that they wanted to go back and spend the weekend if Tressa didn't mind dropping them off when she left to go run her errands.

"Hahhddd . . . Aliiii!" Tressa yelled upstairs from the kitchen. "C'mon if y'all still want me to take y'all to your grandma's house."

Indie asked, "How long y'all gonna be gone, baby?" He was sitting at the island eating a tuna sandwich.

"Not too long. I'mma just drop the boys off at Betty's, then run a few errands and check on some things for the wedding."

"You want me to come?"

"No, it's not that serious. I'm just checking on bridesmaid stuff. I can handle it, baby."

"Okay," he said. "Did you need me to pick up the boys?"

"They spending the night." She did a quick calculation in her head of his original question. "I should be home in about three hours or so and"—she looked him over in a seductive way, licking her lips—"it's me and you, babe."

Indie scoffed, "That's if Betty ain't there when you drop them off. That woman talks a hole in your dome every time you go over there."

Tressa poured herself a glass of juice. "Especially when she's just coming back from church. She'll want to share the whole sermon."

"Word for word," Indie added. "Good thing it's not Sunday."

"I know, baby, but she's just lonely. She don't have anybody but the boys, really." She put the juice back in the fridge.

"Most definitely," Indie agreed. "But, I respect how you go over there and take time out with her in spite of . . . well, you know."

"So what you gonna do while I'm out?"

"Get Hondo set up in that extra room."

Hondo was Indie's handicapped estranged father who was coming to live with them.

The boys came bouncing down the winding staircase, past framed pictures of them at various ages, almost knocking them off the wall.

"I got front," Hadji said, calling dibs.

"Too late," Ali told him. "I called it first yesterday."

"How about a quick tuna fish sandwich before you guys go?"

They both eyed Indie, each other, and then took off for the garage in a race to the car. "Winner gets the front seat," Ali said.

"Y'all know the deal," Tressa said over her shoulder. "Don't fight over no damn front seat, or y'all both going to be riding in the back."

"They too old to be chauffeured," Indie said to Tressa, shaking his head. "You better not have them boys riding in the backseat like they six years old."

Indie was use to being ignored by the twins, unless they wanted something. He didn't have any biological kids of his own, so they were the closest he'd come to any. He'd been engaged to their mother for eight years now and took care of them as if they were his own. He gave them everything they asked for and anything else he felt they should have. He always went to bat for them. But he wasn't their biological father, so nothing he did was ever enough to acquire that close bond.

Tressa knew the boys secretly held a little grudge against Indie for, in their mind, taking the place of Lucky, but she couldn't make them see that they were better off for it. The truth of the matter was that Indie would never try to take the place of their father, and day after day he proved that he loved them more than anything and wanted the best for them. And the reality was that even though Lucky had had chance after chance to be there for them, he hadn't been interested in being a father. In fact, it had been the furthest thing from his mind.

"That's the problem, they too grown now," Tressa told Indie, then asked, "But how're you really feeling about your pops moving in?"

"Yeah, I'm good. Just gotta lay the ground rules down," Indie said.

"You okay? Do you want me to put off my errands to help you with Pops?" she asked.

"It's kinda awkward, but I can handle it."

When Indie was young, his father had walked out on him, his mother, and his sister, leaving him to be the man of the house and provide the best he could for his family. And now his alcoholic father was suffering from a recent bout with liver disease along with a laundry list of health problems. Out of the goodness of his and Tressa's heart, they agreed to take him in to keep a watchful eye on him.

"Well, call me if you need me," Tressa said to Indie after leaning in to give him a kiss on the lips. "Yuck! You taste like fish. See you later. And brush your teeth," she jokingly scolded.

In the car, Ali was in the front and the engine was already running.

"Ma, we gotta get petro soon," he told her, alerting Tressa that they were near empty but mostly to distract her from changing the CD that his brother had put in the player.

"I know. I'm thinking it may be cheaper in the city." Prices where they lived were the worst. "You would think gas would be cheaper out here in the suburbs."

"Ma, it's only a few cents cheaper in the city, nothing really to write home about." Hadji never understood the value of money, especially not other people's money.

"Pennies make dollars, Mr. Warbucks." Tressa glared at him in the rearview mirror.

The traffic wasn't too bad and once they were off the highway Tressa stopped at a gas station that wasn't too far from Betty's house. Without Tressa having to tell him, Ali got out to pump while Hadji got the money from his mother and went inside to pay for the gas. It was understood between the brothers that whoever sat in the front seat pumped and whoever sat in the back went to pay. Tressa used the time to send a couple of text messages. Then she called Betty to make sure she hadn't gone to church. The woman attended church every single Sunday, and prayer service, bible study, and choir rehearsal during the week faithfully.

Betty answered on the second ring. "Praise the Lord."

"Betty, I'm about to drop the boys off, I'm around the corner." Betty loved spending time with her only grandsons and would do anything in her power to help Tressa out. Tressa and Betty had always had a decent relationship. Betty's.

"No problem," Betty told her, "but I want you to come in to see the new drapes I put up."

So much for the clean escape, Tressa thought. She enjoyed talking to Betty but today she had a lot she needed to get knocked out.

Tressa and Betty had an unusual relationship. When she first started dating Lucky, Tressa had mixed feelings about Betty, but words could never express the appreciation she had for the love and assistance Betty provided over the years. Tressa was like a daughter to Betty, and Betty, a surrogate mother to Tressa. When Tressa was fourteen, her mother went to prison for killing her husband. The man had beat her for ten years until Cynthia got the nerve to gun him down while he was sleeping off a hangover. She ended up killing herself in a jail cell, but Tressa and her brother, Taj, never believed that their mother really took her own life. They knew how much she loved them and her committing suicide would have never been an option. Tressa and Betty filled a void for each other. Although it was strange, Betty even treated Tressa's man like a son-in-law.

"What color are the drapes?" she asked, but when she looked up, she saw two black girls follow a white girl to an old blue

Lexus. The white girl got in the passenger side while the driver, a guy, pumped the gas.

One of the teenage black girls, wearing tight jeans and a maroon baby T-shirt, started pointing and screaming into the Lexus. Tressa couldn't make out her words but all the neck rolling and finger pointing going on indicated that it wasn't anything nice.

While the girl in the maroon T-shirt was verbally assaulting the white girl, her friend took it step a further. Reaching into the car, grabbing a handful of blond hair, she snatched the white girl clean through the window. Once on the ground, they started whaling on the poor girl with fists and feet.

"Oh, my goodness!" Tressa was mortified at the trouncing she was witnessing. She didn't know what to do. Should she get out and try to break it up, or just mind her business?

"What's going on?" Betty asked, alarmed at Tressa's outburst.

"Betty, let me call you back. This girl is getting fucked up. Gotta call the police."

"Watch your mouth, girl. Are you okay? Lord, let me pray for her," Betty said.

Tressa knew it was none of her business and normally she would play her position—see no evil; hear no evil—but the way those two girls were hammering down on the defenseless chick was too much to ignore. If she turned a blind eye to it, something tragic might happen to the girl. Besides, if the shoe was on the other foot and she was getting beat up like that, she would have wanted someone to do the same for her.

"911. What's your emergency?"

"I'm at the BP on Eighteenth and Broad Street, and there's a girl out here who needs immediate assistance. She's getting beat up really bad."

"What else can you tell me?"

"What else can I tell you? Send help right away!" Tressa yelled at the operator, then she disconnected the call.

By the time Tressa ended the call, the two black girls had hightailed it out of there in an old red Camry. The dude that had been getting the gas got in the Lexus and pulled off behind them, leaving the injured girl alone on the ground. By then Ali was done pumping gas and opened the door to get back in the car.

Before he was in the car, Hadji asked, "Ma, can I have a few more dollars so I can get something out of the store?" Both of her sons acted as if nothing unusual had taken place.

"Don't you have money?" she asked.

"Yeah, but I wanna save mines though."

"But you wanna spend *mine*, Mr. Warbucks?"

Tressa handed over a five-dollar bill. By this time, the white girl with long, blond hair was limping through the parking lot in bare feet, crying and asking folks in their cars to help her. "Please, can you call the police?" she asked one lady, then another.

She shuffled through the parking lot like a wounded puppy, begging person after person to be rescued. And folks ignored her, treating the battered girl as if she was invisible. Those who did acknowledge her simply shook their heads.

Tressa rolled down the window and after offering the girl a warm smile told her she'd already called the police so help should be on the way.

"I just got out of hospital," the girl said. Tressa then noticed the hospital bracelet on the girl's arm. "I was in there for anxiety and . . ." The girl was shaking like a leaf, and Tressa felt so sorry for her.

"What happened to make them girls whip your tail like that?" Hadji asked.

Tressa gave him the eye, but was reluctant to scold him because she wanted to hear the answer herself.

The helpless girl started to sob. "When my boyfriend pulled up at the pump, the girl in the reddish shirt flicked me off. And I flicked her back. And once I got out to pay for the gas, she and her friend started talking shit to me in the store. I tried to ignore them but when I walked back to the car, they just came out of nowhere and started fighting me."

"Whipped yo' butt is more like it," Hadji said, and zipped his lips when Tressa shot him a look that said, "if you don't shut up you are about to be next."

The white girl had a bruise under her eye that was sure to turn black and blue, along with scrapes and cuts all over her legs.

"Where is your boyfriend?" Tressa asked.

"He's not really my boyfriend. I just met him yesterday."

"Do you need my phone so you can call someone?" Tressa held out her phone. Clearly this wasn't a safe place for her.

"He ain't coming back." Hadji didn't bite his tongue. "And why didn't he even see if you was okay?"

The white girl shrugged her shoulders at Hadji's question as she took the phone from Tressa and began shakily punching numbers.

She was breathing hard and still looking petrified. Tressa imagined the girl's heart was beating a mile a minute even though the fight was over. Tressa looked the girl over. She was wearing tiny shorts, a halter top, and was shoeless. By the way the girl was dressed, Tressa wondered for a split second, if the girl had been hooking and maybe that wasn't her boyfriend, but her pimp or a trick or something. But even if that was the case, the poor girl still didn't deserve to get the beatdown she got. Nobody did.

Without even thinking, Tressa got out of the car and popped the trunk, took a pair of shoes that she used at the gym, and gave them to the battered girl. "Here, put these on," she said, handing the girl the sneakers. The girl was thankful.

Tressa asked Hadji to go get her a bottle of water. He asked if she wanted one too.

"Yeah, baby."

"My cousin is coming to get me," the girl said as she handed the phone back to Tressa.

Just then Tressa's phone rang. "Hello?"

"This is 911. An officer should be there in approximately five minutes. Does the victim need an ambulance?"

"Five minutes?" Tressa said, wondering why in the hell had they not arrived already. Before the operator could continue or offer an excuse, Tressa rolled her eyes, and said, "It wouldn't be a bad idea to have her checked out."

"Ma'am, did you see what happened?" the 911 operator asked.

"No, I did not," Tressa said firmly. "Just hurry and get here, please."

Calling for help was one thing. Being a witness in court was some other shit. Fuck that.

When Tressa hung up the phone, she noticed that the Camry with the two WWE fighters had returned. The two chicks must not be too smart, doubling back like that with no fear. They had to know that the police would be arriving soon.

At the sight of her attackers appearing, the girl cringed and began sobbing again. "Please leave me alone." When they got out of the car, she said, "I didn't do anything to you."

But this time, it appeared that the helpless girl wasn't their target. They were not even paying the girl any attention. It was Tressa who they focused on.

"So, bitch, you wanna help a hoe-ass bitch, huh?" one said. "You wanna be Ms. captain save-a-hoe?"

"You gonna let this white bitch get your black ass beat down just like her, huh?" the other chimed in.

Tressa ignored the disrespectful threats. She had heard worse, and let the remarks roll off her like water off a duck's back. She decided to take the high road, and said, "The police will be here any minute now. If you were smart you would go on ahead and get the hell away from here before you go to jail and get locked up for this dumbass shit."

The bullies acted as if they didn't hear or weren't at all concerned with the possibility of being locked up.

"I'mma teach you about being a good Samaritan, helping hopeless hoes and shit," the girl in the maroon shirt spouted off.

"And I'm gonna teach yo' dumb, bully ass about fucking with my momma," Hadji said. He pulled a switchblade from his pocket, and the six-inch blade sprang out, sharp and shiny.

"If I were you, I'd peel now." Until then Ali had stayed quiet, evaluating the situation, but he had seen enough. "My brother don't have no problems sticking a bitch dumb enough to threaten our mother."

When in the hell did Hadji start carrying knives? Tressa was almost speechless, but not quite. "Get in the car!" she demanded. *"Now!"*

Ali and Hadji did what they were told. They knew they better had. And Tressa got in right behind them.

The police drove in as Tressa was leaving. She took off so abruptly that she never heard when the girl she'd helped thanked her.

5

Toting

The remainder of the ride to the boys' grandmother's house was completely silent. The boys hated when their mother stopped speaking to them; it drove them crazy, especially when they knew she was mad at them. Since leaving the gas station, Tressa kept both hands on the wheel, eyes never leaving the road. She appeared to be focusing on her driving, but Ali knew better.

Once they arrived at Betty's, the volcano erupted. "Get out my damn car right now!" Tressa ordered. "And get yo' ass in that house."

Ali and Hadji looked at each other, the way they always did, for support. They both saw the hot lava flowing from their mother. They wanted to try and defuse the situation before it escalated any further. But it was too late.

"What part did y'all not understand?" Tressa said. "Don't make me take my belt off and beat the skin off you two in the middle of this damn street." She was fuming.

She'd swiveled all the way around in the seat and faced them. Her eyes felt like lasers that could bore a hole through their adolescent bodies. It didn't even matter that she wasn't wearing a belt. The threat was received, loud and clear. They both knew their mother didn't play and would resort to corporal chastisement on the spot when angry.

"But, Ma." Hadji tried his hand at peace-making again, but Tressa shut him down with her laser eyes.

"But nothing," she said.

They marched into their grandmother's house like condemned prisoners with the warden bringing up the rear.

Betty must've been watching from inside the house; the front door opened the moment their feet hit the porch steps.

She greeted them with a big hug. "How are my boys doing?" After the hugs, they all moved inside.

Good, Ali thought. They had an ally, three against one. Maybe that would even the playing field.

Then again, maybe not. Tressa didn't seem to be fazed by the numbers against her.

"These two fools were riding around with me in my car with big-ass machetes like junior Rambos or something!" Then, she turned to the boys, and said, "Gimme the damn knife."

Betty's mouth dropped when Tressa mentioned knives.

Hadji hesitated briefly and then palmed the blade in his pocket and removed it with a lot fewer dramatics then when he flashed it at the female bullies at the gas station.

"What about you?" Now Tressa was talking to Ali. "If Hadji got one," she said, "I know damn well you toting one too."

Ali tried to give her his innocent face, the one that never worked when they were younger. And it still didn't work.

Tressa warned, "Don't play with me, boy." Judging by her eyes, he could see that it was definitely a warning, not a threat.

Ali realized he had limited options: play dumb and take the risk of her shaking him down, which would only make her angrier. Or comply: get it over with and face the music. He chose the latter. He placed the black-handled six-inch switchblade that was indentical to Hadji's on his grandmother's kitchen table.

Betty was still visibly disturbed by all this. It was hard for her to believe that her sweet grandbabies were carrying weapons.

Tressa looked at the blades incredulously. "Where did you get them from?" she asked.

"It ain't that serious," Hadji blurted out without thinking, as usual.

"They taught us how to use them to carve wood when we used to go to Boy Scouts." Ali tried to do damage control without answering his mother's question. She couldn't get mad at the Boy Scouts. And if she did, Ali reasoned, better for her to be upset with a national program than with him and his brother.

Tressa didn't fully buy the story Ali was trying to sell her, but she couldn't prove that he was lying. "I don't give a you-know-what who taught you how to use them. Don't ever bring something like this into my house or my car without telling me again. And you." She looked at Hadji. "What were you thinking when you pulled a knife on that girl?"

"Girl," Betty said. "Oh Lord. Father in heaven help us."

Hadji didn't even have to think about this one. "It was two of them, Ma." He looked her straight in the eyes. "There was no way on God's green earth that I was going to let them jump you like they did that white girl."

It was the right thing to say, at the right time. Tressa tried to conceal it, but a trace of a smile curled the corner of her mouth.

How could she be mad? After all, they were only trying to protect their mother.

"What I'm gonna do with them, Betty? I shouldn't even let them stay." After the partial smile, it was a weak threat; they all knew that she would.

"But I got some business to take care of and not enough time to drive their silly tails all the way back home. Make their butts do some chores: cut the grass or something," Tressa suggested. "But you better believe this ain't over," she said, hard-eyeing Ali and Hadji.

"Don't worry about a thing," Betty told her. "You go ahead and run your errand, and I'll take care of my boys."

"That's what I'm afraid of," Tressa half joked. "By the way, the curtains are really nice."

"You've barely had a chance to notice 'em," Betty complained, wanting Tressa to stay longer.

Tressa smiled, this time more than a trace. "Betty, you know don't much get by me." The drapes were blue and yellow. "They go perfectly with your living room," she said. "Give me a call if the boys do one thing wrong, okay?"

Betty said that she would and not to worry, but Tressa didn't believe her.

Once Tressa left Betty began walking around the house gathering religious artifacts. She placed prayer oil on the boys' foreheads and began a prayer ritual. She didn't want them to turn out like their daddy, so she prayed hard, speaking in tongues. The boys just rolled with their grandma because they knew if they played along with her now, they could get whatever they wanted from her later.

After the makeshift prayer service was over Betty fixed them something to eat. Barbecue chicken, string beans, and macaroni and cheese. Betty loved to see the boys eat, and the boys loved getting their grub on.

Now that Tressa was gone and they'd finished eating, Ali and Hadji needed to get out from under Betty's watchful eyes without arousing her suspicion.

Hadji had an idea. "Grandma, can you make us one of those lemon cakes with the strawberries?" he asked politely, knowing that she never refused them much of anything, especially food.

"It'll take a couple of hours to get it ready," Betty said, already pulling ingredients out. "You sure you got the patience to wait that long?"

"Yes ma'am," Ali rang in. "We love your lemon-strawberry shortcake. And we could wait over at Tommy's house?"

"To stay out of your way while you bake?" Hadji added.

They put on their puppy dog faces, and said in unison, "Pleaaase."

"Don't be gone too long," Betty said. She may not have always been the best parent that she could have been to Lucky when he was in his younger years but it was her mission to make it up with her grandkids.

Both boys smiled. "We promise. We won't." They kissed her on the cheek and headed out the door. Now all they had to do was find Ace and find out what the plan was to get his truck back to him.

Ali and Hadji walked the entire perimeter of the projects, but Ace was nowhere to be found. The last thing they wanted to do was randomly ask people if they had seen him. After all, technically they weren't even from Cyprus Court. People might start to look at them funny and think something was up.

The only person they felt comfortable asking questions like that was Tommy. When they doubled back through the cut, they found their friend chilling in front of his mother's apartment. As usual he was by himself.

When he saw the twins, Tommy cracked a smile. "What's up, my dudes?" They traded fist bumps.

Ali said, "Same soup, different bowl." He'd heard that line in a movie, and it stuck with him. He'd been using it ever since.

Hadji got straight to the point. "Have you seen Ace?"

Tommy nodded. "Yeah, he was out here earlier. Like thirty minutes ago. How come y'all looking for him?"

More often than not when someone asked for Ace it was either for money, drugs, or the police looking to catch him slipping.

Ali peeped the curious expression Tommy was giving off. "I know you don't think we getting high, do you? Ace used to be boys with our daddy."

"I was just wondering." Tommy shrugged. "Let's go to the rec and shoot some hoops. Ace bound to come back through the way before long."

It was as good as any idea, and it beat walking around in circles.

They were ten minutes into the game of horse when low and behold, Ace popped up. He was sporting his ever-present cocky smile.

"You need to work on that left hand of yours a little more," he said to Ali. "Let's take a walk. You don't mind if I borrow your boys for a minute or two, do you, Tommy?"

Tommy shook his head. "It's your world, Ace. I'm good."

Hadji, Ali, and Ace slipped off. The three were barely out of Tommy's earshot when Ace asked, "Where's the truck?"

Hadji was nervous. He hoped that he'd done the right thing. "We moved it out where we live," he said, and went on to tell Ace their reasoning for doing so.

After Hadji finished explaining, Ace said, "Cool. No problem."

Hadji dropped his head "But there's one small problem."

Ace looked worried.

"There's a little damage to your truck. We never drove anything besides a riding lawn mower and a dirt bike before."

"Is it totaled?"

"I wouldn't say totaled but there is damage; we had a small accident."

"Is everything in the truck still intact?"

"For sure, and we even got a cover for it to hide the damage."

"Smart." Ace nodded. "Well, I'mma get up with y'all tomorrow to get the truck back from ya."

"Okay," the boys said, wondering what Ace was going to say when he actually saw the banged-up Escalade.

6

Not My Boys

The boys were back home. Indie was grilling steaks on the George Foreman grill with his special marinade while Tressa worked the tossed salad. His culinary skills on the grill were incomparable. Everybody loved his T-bones, including Ali and Hadji. Tressa didn't even hold it against him for withholding the secret ingredients of the sauce he soaked the meat in overnight. But at least he wasn't wearing the apron he peacocked around the yard during their cookouts with "King of Beef" pompously scripted across the front. The boys had given it to him a few years ago for Father's Day and he wore it faithfully.

"How do you want yours, baby?" Five pieces of the butcher-cut two-inch-thick prime meat sizzled to perfection on the grill. "Medium or medium well?" Indie asked.

He knew Tressa only ate her steak cooked medium well, but he always asked the same question anyhow. She made the mistake, once, of asking why he continuously inquired about something to which he already knew the answer, and Indie graciously replied, "Because women reserve the right to change their mind anytime they want." He shut her up with that one.

"I would like it cooked medium well today," Tressa said sarcastically. "And my salad is done, so what's taking you so long? I would like to have eaten before the pastor arrives for our counseling, and he should be here in the next hour or so."

"Ye of little patience, my dear. One can't rush perfection." He called her sarcasm and raised her one.

Just then, the doorbell rang. They weren't expecting anyone, unless Pastor Jacobs was early for their marriage counseling. At least, she wasn't. "You gonna get that?" Tressa said.

"Why can't you answer it?"

"I can, but I asked you."

Using tongs, Indie removed the food from the grill, placed it on a plate to cool, then washed his hands. He must've not been moving fast enough for whoever was at the door because they rang the bell again.

"Hold your horses!" Indie yelled before making it all the way to the door and opening it. When he did, he was surprised by who was on the other side.

"Sorry to disturb you," an officer said, "but do an Ali and Hadji Shawsdale live here?"

"Who wants to know?" Indie asked. The question sounded a little silly since the officer was in full uniform, but Indie wasn't going to hide the fact that he really didn't care for the police much.

"I'm Officer Cook," the policeman said, "and we have reason to believe that Ali and Hadji may have been involved in an attempted robbery."

"You gotta be fucking kidding me," Indie said, obviously shocked by the officer's statement. "What reason can you possibly have to substantiate this foolishness? My boys haven't robbed anything or anybody."

Tressa was listening to the exchange, getting more outraged by the second, but she let Indie handle it. If the boys had really robbed somebody, the law would be the least of their concerns. After the beatdown, they would have to worry about being grounded until they were eighteen.

Officer Cook said to Indie, "Right now, we have a potential witness that identified both boys, by name, and said they pulled guns on an ice-cream truck owner."

"Ice-cream truck?" Tressa was floored.

Indie had heard enough. "May I see a warrant?" No need to let this go any further if the cop wasn't official.

The officer reluctantly admitted, "The proprietor of the ice-cream truck hasn't pressed charges as of yet. I just wanted to hear Ali and Hadji's version of what happened."

"Let me get this straight." Indie began to sum up the situation: "A Richmond city police officer comes to Henrico County investigating two thirteen-year-old kids for allegations of a supposed crime that may or may not have happened in the first place? Is this correct?"

Officer Cook looked upset that his authority was being questioned, but Indie knew there wasn't much the officer could do about it. Officer Cook was not only out of bounds but also out of his jurisdiction.

"I was hoping we could resolve this informally," Officer Cook tried to reason with them, as if he was actually doing Indie a favor by showing up at his door trying to get his kids to incriminate themselves in a robbery. "The next time I'll take the more formal approach." It was a weak threat, but Officer Cook had to try to save face.

"Do what you want," Indie said, tired of the bullshit. "Just do it somewhere else." He slammed the door shut.

Tressa was glad Indie was home. She didn't think she would've had the resolve to handle the drama as well as he did. The door wasn't closed more than five seconds before Tressa said, "I'm gonna fuck those two up," and started toward Ali and Hadji's room.

Indie stopped her. "Look, before you go in there and blow up, calm down and let me try my hand with them first. This could very well be a misunderstanding," he pointed out.

Tressa wanted to flip out but Indie could always make her calm down, even when her blood was boiling.

"Just hold tight." He was staring into her eyes. "All right?"

At that moment someone rang the doorbell again, and Indie made his way back to the door. This time it was Pastor Jacobs. *What next?* Tressa thought. She wanted to just faint, she was so embarrassed. Her pastor was standing on her porch while Officer Cook sat in a cop car right in front of the house.

"Hey, how you doing, Pastor Jacobs?" Indie seemed unfazed.

"Praise God. I'm blessed." Pastor Jacobs beamed a fake smile, and then asked, "Is everything okay?"

"Yeah," Indie nodded. "It will be. But if you don't mind, we'd like to reschedule. I apologize that you drove all the way out here, but we have a small crisis to deal with, and neither Tressa nor I would be able to focus on the lessons you'd be giving us."

The minister looked like he wanted to pry, but instead said,

"Yes, of course. However, if you need me for anything, I'm only a phone call away."

"Thank you, pastor," Indie said, and shut the door.

"Oh my *God!*"

"Don't start, Tress, it's going to be okay."

"What do you think he thinks about us now?"

"Fuck him. The bible says don't judge, right? I'm sure this isn't the first time he's seen a cop car. I'm sure he's seen worse." Indie shrugged it off. "Now, instead of worrying about him, we should be worrying about our boys. I'm going upstairs to have a talk with them."

"Okay," she conceded. "We'll try it your way first. Then I'mma fuck they asses up."

Indie went up to the boy's room. They were playing Grand Theft Auto on their Xbox. Tressa quietly waited outside their door, trying to eavesdrop.

"Can I speak with you guys for a second?" They kept playing, but Indie gave them a look that said he was serious. Ali took heed and hit the pause button, stopping the game.

"I need to know what happened at the ice-cream truck."

They glared back at him, neither willing to volunteer any information.

"Check it out," Indie tried to explain, "the police just came here accusing you two of robbing an ice-cream truck. I want to hear your side of the story. If you didn't do it, cool. But if you did, I need to know what exactly happened so that I can keep you out of trouble as best I can."

Hadji erupted. "You always come at us trying to pull that daddy shit. We ain't done nothing. And if we did, it wouldn't be none of your business."

Indie was caught off guard by Hadji's outburst.

Ali didn't appear to fully agree with his brother, but he didn't violate the cardinal rule: you don't cross your twin.

Before Indie could respond and put fire under the boys' butts, Tressa decided she had heard enough and burst into the room like a tsunami. "You two must've completely lost your damn mind. You cursing in my house and disrespecting Indie when all he was trying to do was help you."

The belt was swinging now. The big leather one, designated exclusively for ass-whippings. Slicing through the air like Indiana Jones's whip, the first blow caught Hadji on the leg. He winced but didn't cry. Tressa popped him again. This time he showed a little more emotion and his eyes glazed up, but he didn't let the water get any further. After she finished tearing into Hadji's behind she dished the same punishment equally to Ali.

"I'mma give y'all time to get your shit together and then I want to know why in the hell the police was at my door talking about you robbing something. If y'all stupid enough to rob a damn ice-cream truck when neither of you want for anything, you ought to be locked up." Tressa regretted saying the words the moment they flew from her mouth, but she was mad.

After taking a shower and getting herself together, Tressa went to apologize; to give the boys another chance to explain what happened. But they were gone.

7

On Ice

After the bullshit with Indie, the whipping, and drama from their momma, Ali and Hadji couldn't wait to sneak out and get with Ace at the prearranged destination a few blocks over from the house to handle their business.

Once Hadji handed the keys to the Escalade over to Ace, he looked relieved and impressed. He said, "I know it's kinda late but y'all wanna go get something to eat? Take a ride? It's all good. Whatever y'all want to do."

"You on," Ali said, not wanting to go back to the house and face the music.

"I'm up for anything that don't involve going in that house," Hadji agreed.

"Why?" Ace asked Hadji, sensing something was wrong.

"Indie be tripping like he our real daddy or something," Hadji snapped off. "Dude don't know us like that."

Ace smiled, not believing his luck. "You right," he said. "Dude's pedigree ain't nothing like yo' daddy, that's real. Indie grew up on an Indian reservation, selling smokes in the family smoke shop and yo' daddy got his rep in the streets."

"You telling us something we already know," Ali said before eagerly asking, "What happened when the police picked you up? What did they want?"

Ali wanted to change the subject because he didn't think it was right nor did he feel comfortable airing their dirty laundry to Ace . . . or anybody else for that matter.

Hadji seen it differently. "Man, that dude bout to marry our momma and . . ."

Ali dispelled any skepticism about whether twins could really communicate without speaking by barely looking at his brother and conveying the message: "Chill with the Indie bashing out in public." Then he gave his attention to Ace, letting him know he was ready to hear the answer to the question he had just asked.

Ace said, "That's a good question. The chump that grabbed me was named Agent Foster. I couldn't believe the shit when that nigga put a picture of yo' daddy in front of me." Ace looked up from the road at their expression to be sure the twins were paying attention. They were more than intrigued now that he'd mentioned Lucky.

"Agent Foster asked me, 'How well did you know Khalil Foster, aka Lucky?' Then he answered his own question. 'You two were good friends, right?'

"I was thinking, motherfucker, here we go again—like at the Chinese store—asking me shit he already knew the answer to."

Hadji got a little impatient. Ace was taking too long to get to the point. He wanted Ace to cut to the chase. "They think you killed our daddy?"

Ace got crazy-eyed. "You should know better than that, youngin'. Never that! I loved Lucky like a brother."

"Then why would they be bringing up our father's name after all this time?" Ali questioned, unable to find a logical reason why the Feds would bring all that fire power and then show Ace a picture of Lucky unless they thought he was tied up with their father's death.

"Naw, baby boy, they were deep-sea fishing. That's all."

"Fishing for what?" Ali asked. The boys looked at each other curiously.

"Some old-ass shit me and your daddy did back in the day."

"Tell us about it." Hadji never got tired of learning about his biological father.

Ace paused for a second as if he was considering a response. "Naw," he said, "it's some grown-man shit."

"Come on, Ace. Hearing about our dad from people that were closest to him is the only way we're ever going to know 'em. If he was really yo' friend, like you say, then it's your obligation to tell us."

"Who else gone tell us? And it's only fair anyway," Ali added.

"You need to know that this shit can still get me put under somebody's jail. If you ever get caught up repeating what I said, it could end me in a lot of trouble."

"You can trust us," Hadji practically begged. "We won't say anything."

Ace continued the story about the police interrogation, and how it related to the past he shared with Lucky.

"Agent Foster then asked me, 'How about an African by the name of Radda? You remember him?' Then he removed a seven-by-ten glossy photo from a manila envelope he'd been holding. Tossed the picture on the table. 'Maybe this'll help jar your memory,' he said.

"The picture brought back memories that I would have taken to my grave if I wasn't sharing them with you right now. Now, you have to carry it to yours."

"What happened?" They both wanted to know, now, more than ever. Ali and Hadji held their breath waiting for Ace to continue.

"Lucky was excited as a sissy working in a dick factory when he was released from the city jail back then. He'd thought that he would have to do a bid, but it wasn't just his newly returned freedom that had him feeling himself. Lucky ranted on and on about having a lick of a lifetime that was going to make us rich. And how it was going to set us up in the good life. I recall that shit just like it was yesterday," Ace said before mocking Lucky: "'All I have to do is kill one African nigga, and we are set for life,' he said. 'And I need two good soldiers to watch my back.' Lucky was eyeing me and Tre Dog. 'I'll take care of the rest,' he said."

"Who was the African?" Ali asked.

"A filthy rich-ass drug boy that must've pissed off the wrong person."

"So, you were Dad's accomplice?" Ali continued to delve.

Ace nodded. "Me and Tre Dog helped but your dad laid everything out. He studied this guy's moves every day for weeks, putting together the perfect plan. But there were a couple of complications.

"Radda had given his bodyguards the night off while he was out chasing pussy, so snatching him up wasn't a problem." Ace was studying the boys as he spoke and they could both feel it. "If you don't learn nothing else from this story, know this: girls can be a major distraction."

"Momma tell us that all the time," Hadji said.

"But if everything was planned out perfectly, what was the problem?" Ali wanted to know.

"No matter how much something is thought out, there's always a chance of the unexpected." Ace spoke in a tone that was more like teaching than reminiscing. "When we took the African back to his mansion we discovered a small piece of the puzzle that Lucky had somehow overlooked."

"What was that?" Hadji asked.

"Radda didn't live alone. There were two others. We had already laid Radda down on the living-room floor. I had my gun on him so he wouldn't try anything stupid. But while searching the house, Lucky stumbled upon the two unexpected family members. A woman was laying in her bed asleep in nothing but her birthday suit, and the child was beside her. She was a bad bitch too," Ace told them. "Tall, smooth, dark-skinned, high cheekbones, and hair that flowed down to a bodacious butt. A bona fide dimepiece. Dude had to be a fool to cheat on that.

"When the woman opened her eyes she begged in an African accent, 'Please don't kill me, baby,' A natural reaction after waking up with a gun in her face. Her nipples were brick hard too."

"So what did y'all do?" Ali asked.

"Lucky ordered her to get out of the bed with the kid, then walked them to the living room, she still buck naked, and laid them on the floor beside her man."

Ace paused for a moment, studying their faces before he continued.

"See," Ace said, "that's the kind of gangsta your dad was. He didn't panic under pressure. He turned a potential problem into an advantage. The extra edge he needed.

"'Where is the money at?' Lucky demanded. He was talking to Radda, while looking at the woman. The implication was subtle but clear."

"No respectful man would let his family die over some money," Ali said, "would he?"

"Especially not this exotic piece of ass," Ace said with a wink.

"Maybe you wrong, Ali." Hadji wasn't as sure as Ali was about that. "Maybe the African dude ain't care."

"You're right, Hadji, maybe dude didn't," Ace teased. "Radda was stone-still like Lucky hadn't said shit. Now that I think about it he hadn't spoken a word since we'd grabbed 'em."

"So what happened?"

"I'll tell you what happened. Lucky pointed the gun toward the newborn and said, 'I will start with the baby then maybe that will help you find your voice,' The woman screamed at her baby's daddy, 'Don't let them hurt me baby!' Then she demanded that Radda give us what we came for."

"Did he do it?" Hadji pressed.

"At first Radda appeared to be analyzing his options, but it didn't take long for him to make the right decision. I can still remember him saying, "'Just don't kill me fame-lee.'" Ace was shaking his head like he was trying to rid himself of the voice, still.

"See, told you, a real man wouldn't let his family die for money." Then Ali said, "Wait a minute. He didn't kill them, did he?" Ali had heard rumors of his father's unpredictable behavior so he couldn't be sure.

"You know Daddy smoked them fools," Hadji said with his chest poked out.

"Man Daddy ain't kill no baby." Ali looked unnerved by the mere thought of it.

"Baby was in the wrong place, at the wrong time," Hadji said, trying to show off for Ace.

Ace let them go back and forth before he went on. "Lucky's eyes sparkled. For a second, we all thought Radda was going to try to play superman and do something stupid. 'Then tell me where it's at,' Lucky said, with that twinkle in his eyes, 'and be quick about it.'"

"Where was the money?" Hadji couldn't contain his excitement.

"It was in a fake fuse box in the pantry. Turns out the fuse box was an oversized wall safe. But before Radda opened it, he must've knew in his heart that it was over for him. He asked one favor: 'don't hurt me fame-lee,'" in his strong African accent.

"And?" Ali urged Ace to go on.

"Lucky raised the 9 millimeter to Radda's face and pulled the trigger twice. While Radda was laying on the floor Lucky shot him one more time, in the heart. Radda wouldn't have to worry about money, or his family, where Lucky had sent him."

"Dayuuummm," the twins said in unison.

"And by the time Lucky got back to the front of the house with the duffel bags full of money and drugs, the woman was dead too. I'd put her out of her misery." Ace didn't sound remorseful until he shook his head and lamented, "A good piece of pussy gone to waste."

Ali asked the question that both boys wanted to know, "What about the baby?"

"That's when Lucky done some shit I will never forget for as long as I'm on this cesspool called earth," Ace said.

"What?" both inquired, eager to learn how it all ended.

"Lucky looked to me and Tre Dog, then said, 'No witnesses, right?' I ain't say shit because I was on the fence about the baby. I was still fucked up that the lil' fucker was there in the first place. But Tre Dog ain't give a shit either way."

"Stop prolonging," Hadji told Ace. "We trying to find out what happened."

"Just tell us," Ali said.

The suspense was killing them.

"Lucky glaring at the baby said to him, 'It's your lucky day,' scooped the drooling little fucker up and brought him with us."

"What did y'all do with it?"

"We dropped him off at an IHOP and kept it moving. That was the start of your daddy's legend-hood. And there was no turning back."

"So," Ali said, "you never told us what you said to the agent about the whole thing."

"I ain't tell him shit." Ace looked at the boys like they were crazy for insinuating that he would do anything different. Then he cracked. "This wasn't no *Law and Order* episode where the bad guy confesses before the last set of credits roll."

The boys laughed at Ace's oily tongue.

Ace dug in his pocket. "I want to give y'all this." He handed each of them a bankroll. "Thanks for looking out for me, you saved my ass. I could've been in more trouble than you even know."

"It's a bunch of drugs in here, isn't it?" Hadji asked, referring to what they had been hauling around.

"You wanna see?" Ace put the SUV in park. They were two blocks away from the twins' house.

"Naw, man. It's probably better if we don't know," Ali said.

"I think it's better that we know what we co-conspired to," Hadji contradicted.

"Before y'all walk the rest of the way home, let me show y'all real quick." Ace got out of the SUV and the boys followed him to the back.

When he opened up a compartment that was secretly concealed in the floor, there was a huge ice-cooler. But there wasn't anything that could prepare the boys for what they saw when the lid to the cooler was removed.

They almost jumped out of their skin. "Oh shit!" they exclaimed when they saw the cut-up dead body: a torso with the head, arms, and legs cut off and thrown on top of the torso.

Ace told them, "I gotta dump it somewhere." Like it was leftover trash.

Ali and Hadji tried to remain calm. Hadji was on the verge of asking if he needed any help when Ali gave him one of those telepathic looks that said, "Don't fucking think about it."

Hadji asked, "One more question?"

"If you're not careful," Ace said, "you 'gon fuck around and grow up to be a fucking journalist or something." He spat the word as if it was a bad thing, then asked him. "What you want to know?"

"Who killed my father," Hadji bluntly asked. The question landed like a grenade in a mall filled with people.

Ace tried to hide a slight devilish grin, "Are you sure you want to know the answer to that?" Ace licked his lips, somehow knowing that the topic would eventually come up.

Hadji had been wanting to know the answer to this question for as long as he could remember. He hadn't thought about what he would do with the information if he ever found out the truth, but he knew that he wanted to know.

"I'm positive," Hadji said.

Ace looked to Ali and surprisingly Ali said nothing. But like his brother, Ali gave Ace his undivided attention waiting for the answer to the million dollar question.

"According to the streets," Ace said in a subdued voice as if he was showing deference to the dead. "The man that killed your father is. . . ."

In the brief moment it took Ace to complete his sentence an eerie silence filled the night air. Off in the distance, an old owl, wise beyond its years, could be heard in the treetops that insulated the suburban neighborhood. *Wwhhoo! Wwhhooo,* as if he, too, wanted to know what Ace had to say. The twins had no idea how much the answer would impact their lives. For better or worse—depending on who was asked. The seconds that it took Ace to utter the answer to the question at hand seemed like decades to the twins.

"Indie." With that one word the grenade went off. "They say it was Indie who killed Lucky." The indelible damage from the shrapnel . . . devasting.

8

Smelling Themselves

The chorus of "Golden" by Jill Scott blared from Tressa's smart phone. After gropping at the night table in search for the device, she finally found it, and pushed the answer button.

"Hello," she managed to say with her eyes still glued shut. She'd stayed up last night until way past the other side of midnight worrying about Ali and Hadji. Knives? Attempted robbery suspects? Arguing with Indie? Sneaking out of the house? Too much to deal with at once. She still couldn't believe it was all happening.

"Tressa, where are you?" the voice on the end of the phone inquired.

It was Marvin, Eli's press secretary.

"Shit!" Tressa said after rolling over and prying her eyes open. She looked at the clock and couldn't believe that it read 8:35 A.M. She was late!

This was a first. In the two years that she had worked in the mayor's office, there wasn't a day when she hadn't been there at least thirty minutes before her start time, until now.

Tressa apologized. "I'm so sorry. I will be there within the hour. Is everything okay?" she asked.

"Yeah, we're all good. Eli was just wondering where you were. It's not like you to be late," Marvin said.

"I know," Tressa said, disappointed in herself. "I will be there as soon as I can."

"Well, take your time. I can hold the fort down until you arrive. But we both were worried about you. Is everything okay?"

"I'm fine," she said to him. "Eli's schedule is clear until his eleven o'clock meeting with the police chief, and I should be in well before then."

"No need to rush, I will definitely cover for you," Marvin tried to assure her. "Surely that's the least I can do after all the times you've had my back."

"Awww, thanks a lot. But I gotta go. See ya soon." Tressa ended the call as she threw the covers back, hopped out of the bed, and began getting ready. Thirty-five minutes later, she was dressed and prepared to go. She hurried down the hall to the boys' room. Usually she knocked before entering but not this morning. They both were still in dreamland. She pulled both of their sheets off of them and said in a firm tone, "Don't leave this house." She had held back on them last night when they were sneaking back in.

"Until when?" Hadji asked his mother.

"Until further notice," Tressa said, looking at them both closely to be sure that there was no misunderstanding before exiting their room. "I'm not playing."

As she walked through the kitchen to leave the house, she ran into Indie's father. He handed her a stainless steel to-go cup with a top. "Judging by time, you won't be able to stop by Star-bucks so I took the liberty of making you coffee."

"Thanks, Pops. Truly. It's truly appreciated." She grabbed it out of his hand and snatched the bagel that had just popped up from the toaster.

"Wish you had time to stay and have breakfast with me and the boys."

For the few days Hondo had been staying with them, he had been a blessing, helping out with Ali and Hadji—at least up until 3:00 P.M. Once the evening rolled around, she knew it was a wrap. From 3:00 P.M. on, Hondo was drunk as a fish.

"Wish I had time to sit with you and enjoy, but I gotta run. Thanks for the coffee, Pops, and for all this. And I'm sure the boys will love it, though. By the way, I told them not to leave this house for any reason, so don't let them tell you anything differ-ent." She kissed her father-in-law-to-be on the cheek. "Try not to drink too much, Pops."

"I'll try," he said, mostly to himself, as she walked through the door.

Tressa sped through the light traffic to get to work. As soon as she got into the office, she noticed that Eli's door was closed. He usually kept his door open so if he needed something from her he could just call out. His door was rarely ever closed unless he had a meeting or . . . she didn't even want to think about this new habit he had picked up.

That was odd, she thought after looking at her watch and double-checking her calendar against his. Unless something just came up, no meetings were scheduled.

She thought it would be best *not* to announce her arrival in case something had just unexpectedly come up. Instead, she started catching up on e-mails. Eli would call if he needed her.

She was sitting at her desk, trying to focus on the task at hand, but she couldn't help being distracted by what were becoming familiar sounds.

A few "Ohhhhs," in between a couple of moans, and there was no denying that it was Eli's voice she was hearing.

Just thinking about how he was treating Ivy made Tressa sick to her stomach.

"That's right, baby, help daddy get there," she heard Eli say in between grunts.

Whoever his new concubine was, she was putting it on him. After a few more deep moans and deep thrusting sounds things started to fall off his desk.

Dayum, she thought as she tried to suppress her mind from conjuring up images. *Yikes.*

As soon as she got rid of the image of what was going on behind the double doors, she heard what sounded like Eli climaxing. Then without warning, it all suddenly stopped.

A moment later, Eli's voice came across the intercom, "Tressa?"

She had to shake it all off before answering in her professional voice, "Yes?" as if nothing strange had been going on in that office or in her head.

"Will you go grab us some Starbucks please?" he asked, and then placed his order all in the same breath. "I'd like a quad pump mocha venti."

Normally she would have had one of the interns run the errand, but honestly, Tressa was grateful for the opportunity to leave. Anything to limit her knowledge of him having an affair.

She didn't even want to know who the woman was—the less she knew the better off she figured she would be. She tried to tell herself that if she didn't actually see the person, it would give her plausible deniability if push came to shove. She left so quick it felt like she was running from the police, but when she came back, it didn't take Eli long to realize that she was on edge.

He sat on the corner of her desk. "Listen, Tressa, we've been working together for quite some time. And I look at you as one of my sisters. You can share any of your concerns with me."

Tressa had no idea where Eli was going with this. To be honest, Tressa thought he sounded kind of paranoid.

"I'm okay," she said, but her tone must have given her away.

"No, you are not," he said. "I can tell. At least tell me if it has anything to do with me. Is it what you may have overheard this morning? If so, I can explain."

Tressa shook her head. "Of course not." But she wanted to ask her boss, how could a married man of his stature with so much to lose be carrying on in such a manner? And philandering in his office? And just not any office, but the mayor's office? But she didn't ask any of these questions.

"Come on, now, Tressa. I can tell there is something going on that has really gotten under your skin."

"I just had a long night," she said truthfully. Too bad she couldn't say the same for him. "Nothing that will interfere with my work performance."

"Is it the wedding? You're not getting the jitters, are you?" He'd heard her, but he obviously wasn't satisfied with her answer.

"No, not at all." The thought of being Indie's wife brought on an unsummoned smile.

"Well, until you share it with me, I'm going to keep at it."

Tressa gave in somewhat; she wasn't going to get any work done if she didn't. "It's just that my boys are having a really hard time adjusting to the notion that Indie is about to be their stepfather, that's all." Tressa took a deep breath, not wanting to dump her burdens on her boss, but he was being persistent. "It's just a tough transition at their age," she said.

"Oh, I know that age all too well," Eli said. "That's when they start smelling themselves."

Tressa agreed but changed the topic. She was his assistant; she wasn't supposed to be dumping on him. "The chief of police should be here shortly. Do you need anything before he arrives?"

Eli stood up. "The preparations you made yesterday were sufficient."

"Good." Tressa smiled. "But there are a couple of phone calls that you need to make. If you like, you can make those before the chief arrives."

"Good idea," he said, and he began to head back to his office, then stopped in his tracks and came back over to her desk. "Tressa, I've known your boys for a while, and if you like, I could mentor them. Just to kind of get in their heads to see where they are."

Tressa was touched. "That's nice of you, Eli, but you don't have time for something like that."

"I'd make time for them!"

"I'll keep that in mind," she said.

Thirty minutes later, Eli sat on the business side of his desk, wearing a chalk-striped navy blue suit tailored to fit the contour of his six-foot-two-inch frame perfectly, while Chief Donald

Higgins reclined across from him. The two men got right down to business.

"Morale is down among my officers, and crime is up," Chief Higgins started. "That's not a productive combination."

Eli had heard it all before. "What do you want me to do, Donald?"

"I need for you to approve the overtime for my men. They are out there risking their lives twelve hours a day and only get paid for eight. I want you to make it right, Eli."

Eli exhaled. "The city just doesn't have the extra money in the budget to do that, Donald. The economy's so fucked up we can barely keep the trash off the roads, which by the way, those same roads need repairing."

"Well," Chief Higgins shot back, "what do you think will happen to the economy when the citizens stop going to work because they're afraid of either getting mugged or of their houses being robbed while they're out trying to make a living?"

"You're exaggerating, Donald."

"Not by much, Eli."

The mayor was faced with a tough decision, but one that had to be made.

"Listen," Eli said, "I know someone who can help."

"I know, he's sitting across from you," Chief Higgins dug in. "That's what I've been trying to do, *help you*. But I need your assistance to do it."

"I know someone that's got an ear closer to the ground than you and me," Eli continued to try to sound convincing. "Not only does he listen to the streets, he speaks to the streets as well. Isn't it the gangs that are mostly committing all the crime?"

Chief Higgins nodded in agreement. "Most . . . but not all of it," he said.

"Nobody can stop all of the crime, Donald. I'll be satisfied with the numbers going down—by any amount—rather than up."

"I second that. But exactly how do you plan on accomplishing this miracle?"

"Like I said before, I have a friend. Give me thirty days. If nothing has changed by then I'll approve the overtime for your officers."

Chief Higgins agreed to the terms. "But I have one a question," he said.

"Shoot."

"Who is this friend? Does he have a name?"

With a smug smile, Eli said, "That's two questions. Yes, he has a name, but it's probably better for everyone if I keep it to myself."

9

Say Hello to the Bad Guy

The drive was filled with the tension and anxiety of a trip to the dentist's office, only unlike at the dentist's office, there wasn't Novocain to look forward to.

Ali's face was as tight as a size-small pair of latex gloves. "Why do we have to see a shrink? We're not crazy."

"Mr. Thomas isn't a shrink, he's a counselor," Tressa corrected her son. "And I asked him to talk to you about your feelings about the wedding and whatever else you may have on your mind that you feel like discussing with him."

"A counselor, a psychologist, a shrink. It's all the same thing."

Larry Thomas was a social worker that specialized in troubled and at-risk teenagers. At first when the boys started acting a little more antisocial toward Indie than usual Tressa thought that they were just being boys. Although Indie had been with them for seven years, she just assumed that officially getting a stepdaddy was a totally different story in the boys' eyes. But it wasn't until the knife incident and running into Nosey Rosey, who told her about the boys hanging around the neighborhood with Ace, that everything seemed to be speeding out of control.

And Tressa knew she had to do something before the boys crashed and burned. She was pretty sure that the boys wouldn't open up to her or Indie, which left no choice but to seek outside professional help.

Since Larry had a good reputation and was known as one of the best in the area for dealing with this kind of thing, Tressa felt like it wouldn't hurt for Hadji and Ali to speak to him.

"You the one tying the knot," Hadji said from the backseat. "Why don't you talk to him?"

Tressa glimpsed Hadji's sourpuss face in the rearview mirror, a perfect bookend to his brother's. "I'm not the one with pent-up anger, pulling knives, and God only knows what else," Tressa said, trying not to flip on Hadji before getting to the therapist's office. So she responded on a lighter note. "For your information," she said, trying to ease the mood, "Indie and I did schedule an appointment to see a counselor: Pastor Jacobs."

Ali knew that he had to get the conversation back on the right path, because Hadji had definitely rubbed their mother the wrong way and was on the way to getting them both in trouble, so he said, "You mean the same Pastor Jacobs that baptized us when we were younger?"

"Yep." The very one and same. She steered the car into a medium-sized parking lot and stopped in front of a brown, brick building with black-tinted glass windows. "You only have to see the man for forty-five minutes together. I really want you to make the best of this experience. Can you do that for your mother?" She paused for a second. "After almost twenty-four hours of hard labor, surely you can spend forty-five minutes talking to a man for your mother. I'd say that's the least you can do."

Ali sighed and Tressa suppressed the urge to pop him upside the head, then he responded, "Sure, Mom."

That's what Tressa wanted to hear. She turned to see Hadji. "And you?" He tried, unsuccessfully, to avoid her eyes.

He muttered, "Okay."

Hadji spoke so low Tressa nearly didn't hear him. "Good enough," she said. "Let's go." She led them up the walkway, single file, like a mother duck escorting her young ones to the pond.

The receptionist was on the Internet when they walked in. Judging by how fast she killed the screen when Tressa and the boys arrived, it probably had nothing to do with her work. "May I help you?" She was professionally dressed and looked to be in her thirties.

"Hi." Tressa smiled at the lady. "I'm Tressa Shawsdale, and my sons, Ali and Hadji, have an appointment to see Mr. Thomas."

"Yes," she spoke cordially to Tressa, returning the smile. "He's expecting you." The receptionist scooped up the phone from its cradle and punched one of the numbers with a two-inch manicured nail. "Ms. Shawsdale is here with her sons." After hanging up, she said, "Larry will be right out."

Thirty seconds later, a door opened to an office and a man stepped out, wearing blue jeans and a striped button-up shirt. He walked over and shook Tressa's hand. "Good to see you again."

"Likewise," Tressa said with a smile. She had met him a couple of days before, when she went in for the intake meeting during which she shared the backstory and details of what her sons had been doing. Now it was time to introduce the three of them. "This is Mr. Thomas."

Larry extended his hand. "But everybody calls me Larry."

The boys gave him a once-over. He was short, about five-seven, thin build. He looked to be in his early forties.

He said to Tressa, "I would like to speak to Ali and Hadji alone." He winked. "Man to man. You can leave if you want and come back in forty minutes or so, or you can just wait here. We can get you something to drink if you like?"

"Thank you, but I'll be fine. I'm going to just sit here and catch up on some work." She nodded toward her laptop.

The desk in the corner inside of Larry's office was furnished more like a boy's den than a therapist's office. Dallas Cowboys and Yankees memorabilia were scattered about and adorned the walls and bookshelf. He directed the twins, "Have a seat." The twins sat beside each other on a burgundy leather sofa. Larry took a load off across from them in a recliner. "Did either of you catch the game last night? Yankees and Boston? I thought New York was going to lose for sure, down six to three, bottom of the ninth, and then Jeta stepped to the plate . . ."

Neither Hadji nor Ali answered. They'd promised their mother they would *see* the man; no one said anything about speaking.

"I feel you," Larry said to their silence, trying to make light of the awkward moment. "You think I'm the bad guy, huh? Say hello to the bad guy." He was speaking in an Al Pacino-from-*Scarface* voice. "Take a good freaking look."

The poor impersonation was kind of funny, but the twins didn't give him the satisfaction of cracking a smile.

"Your mother tells me she's getting married and you two are a little salty about it. Is this true? Are you upset that you're not going to be the sole attention getter of mother dearest anymore?" The Scarface voice was gone. "You gotta man up, boys. You can't expect her to be single forever. Don't you want her to be happy? Don't you feel she deserves happiness?"

Ali broke the omertà first. "Man, you don't know shit about our mother—or us. So don't sit here trying to play us like you can just pick us for information."

"I know more than you think, son. I've been doing this for twenty years. I know that you've taken up with a known drug-dealing scumbag because you're confused and want someone to talk to. But all you're going to do is end up in a jail cell if you don't tighten up."

If Larry's plan was to earn their respect, he'd failed miserably.

Hadji said, "Man, fuck you!" He looked Larry straight in the face.

"So, you think you're tough." Larry used to work at Beaumont Learning Center for boys, where some of the worst kids in Virginia get off on the wrong foot, so he was used to dealing with disrespectful knuckleheads.

And if it was anything that could rub Larry the wrong way it was the two words "Fuck you."

"Those are awfully strong words coming from someone that probably hasn't even had sex with a girl yet. Prison may be what you need," he said.

Like boiled eggs in a microwave, tempers exploded. It was difficult to distinguish the adult from the children.

The twins talked smack to Larry for fifteen minutes straight; they lambasted him about his receding hairline, how the Cowboys suck and couldn't win a playoff game with Romo, the Yankees losing the World Series to the Red Sox, and his crooked nose.

They were actually having fun. What could he do about it? Put them out?

"I tell you what," Larry finally said. "I'll give one of you a free punch at me because you seem so angry, it may do you some good to get it off your chest." Larry had used this same tactic before with other children. Sometimes the strategy worked to calm down the child and demonstrate who was the alpha male of the group. He used to box in college and had never been knocked out. "Deal? After that we talk the remainder of the time like civilized men. How bout it? You may even learn something."

Hadji and Ali locked eyes. They had never hit a grown man before and the invitation to do so was very enticing. Larry remained sitting in the chair across from them with a confident smirk. "Deal," Hadji said. He wanted to knock that very smile right off Larry's face.

Larry stood up. "So the deal is one punch to my face, then we talk. Which of you wants the free shot?" he said.

Of course Hadji was who stepped up. "That'll be me."

With his chin poked out, Larry braced for the punch. Hadji balled his fist tight and took another look at his brother. Ali nodded.

Larry observed that Hadji was more nervous than he thought he would be, so he taunted him. "Come on, you little momma's boy." And that was all it took for Hadji to take the swing.

Hadji caught Larry off guard by drop-kicking him like the Dow Jones during the worst days of the recession. Ali watched him go down and curl into a fetal position on the carpeted floor.

Hadji could have sworn he felt Larry's family jewels crush from the striker kick to the groin. He never even saw it coming.

Mr. Tough Guy. He didn't look so tough now with his eyes rolling to the back of his head.

From the floor, Larry started making a chopping motion with his hand by his neck.

"What do you think he's trying to say?" Hadji asked.

Ali took a closer look. "I believe he's saying the session is over." Then he walked over to where Larry was trying to get himself together. "Thanks for nothing and I'm sure there won't be another one and you betta not bill our mother." They left his office.

Hadji and Ali made it out to the reception area where their mother was waiting. Tressa looked up from her laptop and saw the boys. "How did it go?" she asked.

"Everything went well. He said he'll call you," Hadji said as they walked toward the exit.

Ali held the door for Tressa. "Honestly, Mom, I really don't think this is the right person for us. I don't think he likes us."

10

21 Questions

Tressa sat at the vanity touching up her makeup while Indie surfed the television channels on the cable. "Today is the day we start to prepare for the big day, huh?" He tried to sound casual, but Tressa could tell he was a little nervous about the marriage counseling.

"Don't tell me you're getting cold feet," she teased, sneaking a peek at Indie's reflection in the mirror as he abused the remote. "The last thing I need while standing at the altar is a runaway husband."

Indie turned his focus from the television toward her, but Tressa acted as if she didn't notice and continued to apply her eye shadow. "I never ran from anything in my life, babe." Her comment must've touched a nerve. "And I would stand in front of a firing squad before I'd ever abandon you."

Tressa thought his comment was sweet, but the best part about it was that she knew Indie was being honest and not just saying what he thought she wanted to hear. Honesty and loyalty were among his greatest qualities. But that didn't mean she was going to let him off easy. "I hope you're not comparing our wedding day to standing in front of a firing squad," she poked at him in fun.

In the mirror, she could see him coming her way. He kissed her on the back of her neck.

"Of course not," he whispered, gracing her with another kiss. "Don't be so hard on me."

She was about to torture him a little more when someone rang the doorbell.

"That's Pastor Jacobs," Tressa said, looking at the clock on the night table. "He's right on time."

Tressa led the pastor to the great room, which was one of Tressa's favorite rooms in their 5500-square-foot home. The vaulted ceiling and the sparkling chandelier gave the room an elegant veneer but Tressa went out of the way to make sure the space was also comfortable. She wanted it to feel welcoming, not stuffy. The goal was accomplished.

In preparation for today, Pastor Jacobs had given each of them a questionnaire to fill out. He had the papers in his hands now and was reading over them.

"You guys have been engaged for quite some time," he said, placing the notes in his lap.

"Eight years," Indie confirmed.

The pastor asked, "Do you mind telling me why you waited so long?"

Tressa and Indie looked at each other, unsure of whom the pastor had posed the question to. "I don't care who answers," Pastor Jacobs said.

"Well"—Tressa stepped up to the plate to Indie's relief—"we never really thought it was the right time."

Pastor Jacobs nodded. "Then why do you think now is the right time? And whose idea was it to finally make it happen?"

Indie assisted his wife-to-be with this one. "We both decided together," he said. "To be honest, it wasn't really a decision. It was more like a feeling, you know. It felt right to do it now."

Pastor Jacobs seemed to like this response, Tressa noticed. "Do you have any children, Indie?" The pastor wasn't wasting a lot of time getting to the good parts.

"Besides the twins?" Indie said. "No, I don't. But I care for Ali and Hadji as if they were my own."

"How do the boys feel toward you?" Pastor Jacobs asked Indie.

That was another story all together, Tressa thought. It wasn't that the boys didn't like Indie. When Ali and Hadji were younger Indie used to take them everywhere: Kings Dominion, Water Country, Busch Gardens, fishing. It wasn't until recently that they started acting out. Indie tried not to let it get to him, but Tressa knew it was hard.

Tressa answered, "The twins love Indie as much as any thirteen-year-old boys are willing to show, I guess. Like any parental relationship, they have their up and down moments."

The pastor seemed willing to accept this as a valid answer and moved on. "Good. Do you plan to have more children with Indie?" he said.

"We haven't really planned it," Tressa said, "but we're not doing anything to prevent it either." She blushed, feeling uncomfortable talking to Pastor Jacobs about their sex life.

"So, if it happens, it happens, is what you are saying?" Pastor Jacobs qualified.

"Correct," she said with no further input, glad he didn't give them a stern talking to about their pre-marital sex life.

Moving on, Pastor Jacobs said, "I normally spend a lot of time talking about money issues. You know, who's making it and who's spending it. Money is one of the biggest—if not *the* biggest—reasons for divorce today. But I don't think you two are really having any problems in that area by the looks of things." He glanced up from the glasses that were perched on the tip of his nose.

"We do have one rule," Tressa offered.

"And what is that?" The pastor seemed anxious to hear it.

Tressa eyed Indie; they'd had a few discussions about this actually. "Neither of us is supposed to make a purchase for more than five hundred dollars without checking with the other first, as a sort of check and balance," she said.

"Does it work?" Pastor Jacobs asked with apparent interest in the answer.

"Most of the time," Indie said. "Tressa's mainly a shoe girl and she can usually squeeze them in under the five-hundred-dollar bar. Although she shows no discretion about how many pairs she buys."

"Don't make me start about your electronics and gadgets," Tressa shot back, unwilling to take the weight alone.

"My wife is the same way," Pastor Jacobs said with a smile, clearly taking Indie's side. "Are there any other issues concerning money you want to talk about, either of you?"

"No, we're pretty good on that," Indie said, and Tressa nodded her head in agreement.

After more than ten minutes of further questioning on various topics, Pastor Jacob asked them about Indie's dad moving in. "How's that going?"

Indie had never forgiven his father for being a coward and running out on him, his sister (four years younger than Indie), and his mother, leaving them alone to fend for themselves when Indie was only fourteen. Indie had assumed the position of man of the house from that point on—and did a good job of it. He had been street smart and didn't mind getting his hands dirty (legal or illegal). Whatever it took to pay the bills and put food in their mouths.

Recently, Indie's father, Hondo, was involved in a life-changing accident while driving intoxicated. Fortunately, the other car was unoccupied. Unfortunately, for Hondo, he totaled his car and lost both of his legs, and was now suffering from liver issues. "Should've lost his life," Indie said when he first heard about the accident.

With no insurance and no way to support himself, Hondo came looking to his estranged son for help. They'd just gotten the call a few days ago and now Hondo was staying with them until he was back on his feet.

"It's going . . ." Indie said with a sigh. "Nothing to write home about." And that was all he had to say about the man.

The pastor jotted something down on his notes and then commented about how dealing with teenage boys and caretaking of a disabled parent could potentially be a major strain on a marriage, especially a new one. "Are you sure you are up for the job?" he asked, looking right at Indie.

"I'm only sure of one thing," Indie replied, "and that is that I love this woman." The love was visible in Indie's eyes, and his voice. "I've learned that no one can completely plan life; we can only plan for life. And I plan to spend the rest of my life with Tressa."

Pastor Jacobs appeared unsure if Indie was speaking to him or his future wife. But the pastor knew that enough had been said on the subject.

Pastor Jacobs stood. "Then that'll do it for today. Unless you have anything else you want to ask me?" he said, making eye contact with Indie, then Tressa.

"I think we're good," they said at the same time, starting to sound like the twins as they both prayed that the pastor wouldn't ask them to explain why the police was at their house the last time he came to counsel them.

"I'll see you next week," Pastor Jacobs said after they walked to the front door.

They closed the door behind him, unaware of the problems ahead.

11

Murderous Thoughts

The morning crept on to afternoon and the afternoon dragged into evening. Indie was out checking on the progress of renovations being done to a couple of his properties; along with a few other ventures, he flipped houses for a living. Tressa was still at work and had called home three times, already making sure Ali and Hadji hadn't sneaked out or done anything stupid, as she'd put it, like rob an armored truck.

The boys did feel bad about causing their mother to lose sleep after they'd slid out of the house to meet Ace. But if they had the opportunity to rethink the decision, they would've done it the same way all over again. The night out with Ace was perfect in their eyes. Ace didn't deal with them like they were little kids. He treated them with respect—like young adults—and let them make big-boy decisions. Adults didn't get put on punishment for making mistakes.

Being stuck in the house made the boys feel like the walls were closing in. It didn't matter that they had more than a hundred video games for their PlayStation and Xbox, not to mention more than five hundred channels on the television and countless movies on DVD, they couldn't stay busy enough to keep the pressing questions out of their heads: Did Indie really kill Lucky? Did Indie kill their father because he wanted their mother? And was she cheating with Indie while their father was living? If Indie didn't kill him, then why would Ace have made it up?

Hadji looked at his brother. He'd made up his mind. "I think Indie did it." He then asked Ali, "What about you? What do you think?"

That was the problem: Ali wasn't sure what he thought. He'd contemplated the question ever since Ace had uttered the words. "I'm still not sure," he said. "But if Indie is responsible . . ." Ali left the indictment hanging.

Hadji didn't. "An eye for an eye," he finished what he was positive his brother was saying.

For a moment after that neither of them said anything. Ali knew exactly what his brother meant by the biblical reference, "An eye for an eye," but he slowly murmured the words just to hear them out loud.

"You want to kill Indie's dad?" It was crazy, but so was what Indie had done to Lucky. "The man doesn't even have any legs already," Ali pointed out.

Ice-cold, Hadji, said, "All that means is that we won't have to worry about him running."

"I don't know man." Ali wasn't fully on board with this particular idea.

"The bible says an eye for an eye, right? And Indie killed daddy so it's only right for us to return the favor. We can't go throw a football with our daddy, ask him for shit, or go nowhere with him. Nothing we do can get our daddy back."

Things are moving too fast, Ali thought. They'd gone from playing Madden to contemplating the murder of Hondo. "If we do it, and I'm not saying we are or should, but if . . . how do you kill a house guest in your own house and make it appear to be an accident?"

The answer to their quandary was "very carefully." If not, there would be plenty of time to figure out what went wrong while rotting in a prison.

Just like that, a few wild thoughts had transformed into a crazy idea, and that crazy idea had quickly evolved into a strategy to get away with murder. . . .

Hondo was as intoxicated as a sailor in a whorehouse who had just returned from a twelve-month stint at sea. It was half past three, and he'd gotten an earlier than usual start with the bottle.

Sitting in his wheelchair, singing traditional Indian songs, Hondo gripped the bottle of gin he was holding like he was trying to choke the life out of it. Flipping the bird, he guzzled another thirsty swig. Excess booze dribbled down his chin. There was no doubt Hondo was ripped out of his own mind.

Hondo was a drunken bastard way before the car crash. The accident had only made him into a legless one, which didn't change the fact in the eyes of the wife and two kids he'd deserted that he was, and still is, a no-good bum. And no amount of alcohol could camoflauge or change that.

The funny part, if there was one, was that even to this day Hondo didn't know why he'd left his family. He may not have been able to provide everything his family always wanted but when he was there he did a better-than-average job at supplying them for their needs.

How does a man get bored with his own family? Hondo asked himself before turning up the bottle again. *My only son. I should've been there.*

"He's toasted," Ali said to Hadji, almost feeling sorry for him. The two were sitting on the stairs, out of sight, watching Hondo navigate clumsily around the first floor. "You sure we should do this?"

"Yeah," Hadji confirmed with no hint of reservation in his voice. "I'm sure."

Together, the boys watched Hondo roll his chair over to the entertainment wall. Indie had had the cabinetry built to divide the enormous great room into two smaller rooms. It almost reached the ceiling and ran the length of the room. The side Tressa used most doubled as a homework room and a library. The shelves were filled with books, knickknacks, vases, and silver-framed photos. It wasn't a coincidence that Indie preferred the side he coined "the media room," with the big-screen television and hi-tech music and video system.

Hondo was exactly where they wanted him, and Ali and Hadji took full advantage of it as they made their move.

Hondo noticed a particular picture on the shelf. The photographer had captured three people: Indie, his daughter, Reka, and his wife, Maria. Maria had passed three years ago from cancer.

Hondo had never seen the picture before. Apparently it had been taken after he left. Indie looked to be about fourteen or fifteen in the photo, taller and more filled out than he'd been before Hondo had split. Indie posed proudly, chest poked out as if he had already assumed the responsibility and title of man of the house.

Hondo was mesmerized by the photo and wanted a closer look. He tried to grab the frame but it was out of his reach. He inched his wheelchair closer to the cabinet and stretched . . . the frame was still a couple of inches away. He was determined to reach the picture and continued to stretch for it.

Shit!

He sat the bottle of gin down and tried again. This time he used his left hand to push himself up out of the chair a little while reaching for the picture with his right.

The maneuver was working. Just a little closer.

Using his upper-body strength, he was totally out of the chair and he almost had the photo in his hand. Then Hondo heard something move. The last thing he saw after hearing the noise was the entire upper part of the cabinet collapsing on his frail body.

Oh Shit!

12

Praying for the Best

Tressa left work immediately after Indie called her with the dreadful news about Hondo's accident. He said it wasn't necessary for her to come to the hospital, but she couldn't imagine being anywhere else.

When she arrived at the Medical College of Virginia, Indie was standing outside of the ICU. "Is he going to be okay?" Tressa asked before hugging him to comfort him.

Over Indie's shoulder she saw that Hondo was hooked up to a group of machines. "I didn't know it was this bad," Indie told her. "The shelf in the great room fell on him." But Hondo looked like he'd been run over by a bus twice.

"Oh, my," Tressa said, searching Indie's face for emotion, but Indie was a blank canvas.

"The doctors don't know for sure if he'll recover. They don't want to give any false hope. The truth is, Hondo's body, what's left of it, is so deteriorated from so many years of drinking that it may not be strong enough to heal itself. Right now, the only thing they know for certain is that he has two fractured ribs

and a punctured lung. Everything else is just minor abrasions."
Indie was stoic; his russet face and dark eyes didn't give up any
of his feelings.

"He's going to pull through, Indie. I believe that," Tressa
said. "Your father is strong like you."

"He's nothing like me," Indie hissed with a trace of anger,
the first emotion he'd shown since Tressa arrived. "Look, ain't
no need to pretend, so let's be clear: Hondo is nothing but a
drunk and a coward. And if he had any balls I'd take my knife
and cut them off myself. The only reason I allowed him to come
and stay in our home is because of you and my mother.

"My mother was the most compassionate person I'd ever
known"—until you, of course—and I know she wouldn't have
wanted me to turn my back on my father, especially in that
condition . . . like he did to his own family."

Tressa knew that Indie resented his father for running out
but she never knew how deep the hatred was rooted. This was
the very reason Indie made himself into everything his father
lacked: a dependable and responsible family man.

Tressa held Indie's hand. "Your mother was a very smart
woman. I think I know why she wouldn't have wanted you to
abandon Hondo in his time of need."

Indie was curious. "I'm listening," he said.

"Because if you turned your back on him, you would be no
better than him. She raised you better than that, that's why."

Indie hugged her. "That's why I thank God every night for
putting you in my life. You're one of the strongest people I've
ever known."

The doctor came out of Hondo's room and told Tressa and
Indie that there was no real need for them to remain at the

hospital. "There's no way he'll wake up tonight with the pain medicine we've given him."

As they were exiting the hospital Tressa asked Indie a question that had been troubling her. "How did the cabinet fall on Hondo in the first place?"

"When I walked in the house, it was just laying on top of him," Indie said.

Tressa thought about it. "It couldn't have just fallen over. What do you think he was doing?"

"I'm guessing with that heavy unit being in so many pieces, maybe one of the brackets worked its way loose or was defective. I'm going to get to the bottom of it. But all I know is that he was holding that picture of me, Ma, and Reka when I pulled him from under the mess."

"Where were the boys? I told them not to leave the house," she said.

"And they didn't." Indie and Tressa took the elevator to the parking deck together. Her car was near the front. "They were in bed with their headphones on. Slept through the whole thing."

Tressa beat Indie home. The first thing Tressa did was check on Ali and Hadji. They both looked a little odd when she walked into their room. She couldn't put her finger on exactly what it was, but she knew those two better than they knew themselves and she had a gut feeling that something was going on with them.

"Is Hondo all right?" Ali asked after a few moments of awkward silence.

"The doctors aren't sure yet. He was asleep when we left,"

she told them. Hadji could barely look her in the face. "Is there something I need to know?"

Ali and Hadji were acting the way they did when they were younger and had broken something but were trying, not very well, to keep it a secret.

"What you talking about, Ma?"

It was official: Hadji only used that Arnold line from *Different Strokes* when he had done something wrong.

Tressa was sure that the boys had been up to no good but with all her heart she didn't want to believe they had anything to do with what had happened to Hondo. She refused to believe that her children could be that evil. But regardless of how much she wanted to deny it, the truth would not change. She had to find out the truth even if she didn't really want to know.

"I know you two had something to do with what happened to Hondo," she said. She looked at her sons and neither of them denied the accusation she'd made. "I just want you to tell me the truth: did you do it?"

Tressa was expecting them to play dumb, but was surprised by what she saw on their faces. They looked relieved that she had figured it out.

Ali spoke first. "We got something we need to tell you."

His co-conspirator was nodding.

Tressa knew her sons, and whatever had made them do what they did was really bothering them. "Well," she said, "I'm listening."

Hadji shocked her when he said, "We found out who killed our father."

Tressa's breath got caught in her chest like somebody was squeezing the life out of her. Prior to walking into the boys' room, she thought she was prepared for anything . . . anything but this. She stammered, "Wh-what did you just say?" After composing herself she asked, "How did you find out?"

Hadji said, "From the streets."

Tressa was smart enough to know that by *the streets* they meant Ace. Less than a handful of people knew what really happened to Lucky, and Ace wasn't one them. But that didn't stop him or others from assuming. And unlike in a court of law, in the streets, most times an assumption was all it took. She felt like someone had dug up the dead family dog from the backyard and threw it on the kitchen table. Her sons were waiting . . . waiting for her to ask the next logical question. "Who did 'the streets' tell you they thought was responsible?"

Tressa couldn't believe she was having this conversation, in her house, with her sons. But she was. She prayed and hoped that this day would never come, but it did!

Then it got worse.

Hadji said what she had dreaded he might say. "It was Indie."

"Indie," she repeated as if what Hadji said was ludicrous.

Ali and Hadji must've read in her face that she wasn't as shocked as they felt she should've been. Tressa had never been a good actress.

Ali, always the wise one, said, "You already knew." It was an accusation, not a question.

It was no use trying to deny it. Ali and Hadji knew her almost as well as she did them.

"How could you be with someone that killed our father?" Hadji said furiously, raising his voice at his mother for the first time ever in his life. Tressa was surprised and wondered how she went from being the interrogator to the interrogated.

Tressa looked into Ali's eyes. He wanted her to say that it wasn't so.

"Ma, you crossed our daddy for that moccasin-wearing, lame-ass dude," Hadji said.

"Watch yo' mouth! And turn the volume of your voice down," Tressa demanded, giving Hadji a stormy look. Regardless of what they thought they knew, she was still their mother.

"So, now you going to protect him?" Hadji fired back in a volume a couple of notches lower.

"Ma, please, all we want is for you to tell us what happened. Because it's so confusing. . . . We are hearing this and that in the streets, and what else are we to believe, if you never tell us what happened?" Ali spoke to his mother in a respectful tone. "Ma, if what we heard isn't true then tell us what is. It's obvious that you know more than you told us."

Tressa took a deep breath, not really knowing what to say, but she knew she had to say something because things had clearly gotten way out of control in a hurry. She started with, "It's a long story." That was an understatement if there ever was one, she thought. "But before I go any further, I need to tell you that your father wasn't the good guy you may think you remember him as. This isn't something I looked forward to having to tell you. However, it seems I have no choice."

"We're listening," Ali said to his mother while signaling to his brother to slow his roll.

Tressa continued. "Contrary to what you may think or believe, Lucky was a very violent and abusive man. I put up with him as long as I could. When I finally had enough of his cruelty and killing sprees, I packed up you two along with a few things and just left. I couldn't have you two around his madness. I felt like he would have eventually harmed me, maybe even killed me, if I'd stayed. Plus, I had you to think about. You were only two years old then."

Both boys sat there in silence. The floor was hers.

"But the abuse didn't stop when I left him," Tressa told them. It was the hardest thing she ever had to explain to her sons. It tore at the very essence of her sensibilities. Yet reliving the events of the past, in her mind, was almost as difficult for her.

Hadji didn't want to believe what his mother was saying about his father. To him, it seemed like she was talking in circles. "So, you are admitting that Indie killed dad, so he could have you."

"No, that's not what I'm saying. As a matter of fact, your father tried to kill Indie, and ended up killing your Aunt Wiggles in the process."

"Wasn't Aunt Wiggles a crackhead?" Hadji said as if it justified her being killed.

"So since Daddy missed, Indie killed him," Ali asked, trying to get to the bottom of it.

"No," Tressa said. "That's not what happened."

"Ma, please just tell us. We're old enough to handle what happened. We only want to know, so we can have closure."

"Indie didn't kill your father."

"Who did?" Ali asked.

"Why are you protecting him?" Hadji wanted an answer.

"I'm not protecting Indie, but I don't feel you should be blaming him. Lucky was the one trying to kill him. And in fact, Lucky thought he had killed Indie."

"Maybe Indie felt like it was kill or be killed," Ali said in the way that only a boy wise beyond his years could say.

"No, baby." Tressa shook her head trying to convince the boys that they were wrong. She looked into Ali's eyes and tried to make him believe the words that were coming out of her mouth. "Your father put me through so much and there were times I wanted to never let him see you two again, but it was Indie who stopped me. He always reminded me that he knew firsthand how important it was that you boys didn't grow up without your father."

Tressa tried to read Ali's face, and it seemed like she was finally getting through to her sons. If she wanted any kind of peace in the house, her life, and her relationship, she would have to totally convince both of her sons that Indie had nothing to do with Lucky's death. Just when she thought that she had them convinced, Hadji blurted, "Did you do it?"

"Are you serious?" She was shocked that her kids could be so bold to ask her such a question.

"Mom, the only way you could be so sure Indie wasn't responsible is if you knew who did. Were you there?"

That question hit her in the face like a ton of bricks. She wanted to tell them what had really happened on that day, but she knew she didn't dare. She would take that information to the grave, and besides, these were her thirteen-year-old babies, and kids were not supposed to be dealing with issues of this magnitude. Before answering, she thought about what Taj told her a long time ago. It was a rule he lived by: never admit to nothing that can incriminate you. But she knew she had to tell her boys something. So she lied.

"Listen, I don't know what really happened myself. All I do know is that the last time I heard from Lucky he called me and said he was in trouble." Tressa took a deep breath and tried to sound as convincing as she could. "He asked me for help, and I didn't give it to him." She shrugged her shoulders.

"I hate you!" Hadji screamed while tears came to Ali's eyes. "I hate you!" Hadji repeated to his mother. "If it wasn't for you, my daddy would still be here."

Those words pierced through Tressa like they'd been shot from a crossbow into a straw target. It was the truth and it hurt because she saw how much her actions were truly hurting her boys.

"My daddy needed your help, and you didn't help him." Hadji spoke his mind, while Ali looked on, tears rolling down his face.

Tressa flipped out. "Help him? Why would I help that sorry-ass motherfucker? He ain't do a gotdamn thing to make my life or your life easier. Now, I've tried to keep the negative things about your daddy concealed, but you know what? Let me give your ungrateful ass the fucking rundown." Tears came to Tressa's eyes now. "Do you know how many times I begged for him to help me take care of you? Not for extra stuff. I'm talking about for food to feed and give nourishment to your body."

Tressa screamed at the top of her lungs, which shut Hadji up for a minute. He listened as she explained her version of what went down seven years ago. "That motherfucker told me to scram . . . and get it the best way I know how. Alone! With no help from him. And I did everything I could to feed you. I damn near broke my back to take care of you. When I left he never gave me shit for you"—she pointed to both of them— "but a hard time in a living hell. And you want to know why I ain't helped him? Honestly I hoped that motherfucker died a slow, painful death. I didn't care if someone fed him to the sharks. He left me and both of you for dead. We didn't deserve that—under any circumstances."

Since Ace seemed to be more revealing and open about his interactions with Lucky, Hadji chose to believe Ace over his mother.

"I hate you. You spent all his money and then you left him. And you still had money when you left. You just spent it on what you wanted to."

Tressa was furious. She could not believe that Ace was filling her children's heads with bad information. "That's a lie," she said. "I don't know where in the hell you got that shit from."

"A source that was close to my father."

"Fuck your source and the streets, I'm telling you . . . he did nothing for you!"

As Tressa and Hadji went back and forth, Ali kept his thoughts to himself.

"You didn't help him, so you might as well have killed him. I hate you with a passion," Hadji screamed back at his mother. "And I don't wanna live here no more. You should have taken into consideration that it would affect us. You fucked up our lives!"

"Is you crazy?" Tressa exclaimed. It took everything in her not to knock the living snot out of him.

"I'm moving out!" Hadji announced.

"Move then, if you think somebody can take care of you better than I have. Then carry your ass on out! You will see it ain't easy. And nobody is gonna love you like me. Believe that!"

13

Amen

Tressa's attempt to explain the unexplainable only further convinced her sons of her guilt by association.

There wasn't a doubt in either of their impressionable minds that Tressa was trying to paint Lucky out to be the bad guy in order to cover for Indie's true motives. They weren't exactly sure what those motives were yet, but that didn't matter. They'd made up their minds.

Not over their dead bodies would they spend another night under the same roof with the man who murdered their father. And since Tressa had obviously already chosen Indie over them, in their minds, they were left with no choice but to move out.

Although their young lives had yet to give them an experience to which to compare the hurt they felt for their mother when she cried and begged them to believe her, it also hadn't given them an experience to compare to the betrayal they felt by her when she said she had not helped their father when he reached out for help.

The brothers' first disagreement came when Hadji suggested

that they call Betty to come get them. "We need a ride and a place to stay," Hadji argued.

For now, the best idea probably was for them to stay at Betty's. But Ali wasn't sure about how they should tell her why they were moving out . . . or exactly how much they should tell her.

"We got the money that Ace gave us," he reminded Hadji. "Let's just catch a cab to Grandma's. That way, at least we won't have to explain anything over the phone."

Hadji had no argument for Ali's idea.

But once Ali and Hadji got dropped off at Betty's, the questions began. For starters, Betty wanted to know: Why they carrying those big suitcases? Why hadn't Tressa called to let her know why they were coming? And what were they doing showing up in a cab so late at night?

Hadji, against his brother's advice, spilled the beans. *Now the shit is really gonna hit the fan,* Ali thought. Things were beginning to snowball out of control. Regardless of how upset and disappointed Ali was at his mother he knew he wouldn't be able to forgive himself if he or Hadji assisted in getting Tressa locked up for any length of time as a conspirator in Lucky's death.

"We really don't have any proof," Ali said, trying to slow down the potential avalanche. He failed to mention that Tressa had kind of validated the story. Hadji gave Ali an odd look but didn't say anything. He reluctantly decided to let his brother do it his way. Ali continued. "All we know is what we heard in the street." But to assure his grandmother that they weren't completely crazy, he added, "But when we questioned Indie about the rumor . . . he didn't deny it." A small lie, but one that was needed for now, to protect their mother. What if Tressa was telling the truth when she said Lucky would have killed her? Ali felt like it was just all a confusing mess.

Betty called Tressa to get to the bottom of this.

Tressa answered on the first ring.

"Lord have mercy, I'm glad I caught you," Betty said. "God only knows I need someone to explain to me what's going on."

Tressa told Betty about the boys' accusations. "I have no idea where it came from," she said.

Betty convinced Tressa that it was probably best to let Ali and Hadji stay with her for a while. "At least until they calm down some. Besides," Betty reasoned, "it's summertime. You and Indie could use the break." She added, "I know the boys could."

Tressa didn't argue. She told Betty that she was a blessing, and that she didn't know what she would do without her.

Before ending the call and assuring Tressa everything would be fine, Betty said, "I can only do what the Lord allows me to do. Amen."

14

Say What?

How could this shit have gone so wrong so fast? Tressa thought as she tried to figure out how she would explain to Indie what had taken place. She wasn't sure how he would take it. Would he hate her boys? Would he still want to marry her? And how could she blame him? This entire situation had the potential to be life shattering for everyone—Tressa, Indie, and her sons—and there was no way to get around it.

Indie walked into the house, and under the circumstances, he was in a pretty good mood. He was carrying two bags of Chinese food and he laid a big kiss on Tressa's lips.

"Baby, what's wrong?" He could feel that something other than Hondo's well-being weighed on her.

Tressa started crying. "I don't know where to begin."

In between her sobbing, she broke down and told Indie that Ali and Hadji were responsible for Hondo being in intensive care, and how they considered it an act of retribution for Indie's involvement in their father's death.

Indie seemed to take the news much better than Tressa had expected.

"A part of me is actually proud of the boys for doing what they did," he told her, which totally threw her off. She wasn't sure if he had really heard what she had told him. "They did the same thing I probably would've done if I was in their situation."

"I'm sure you'll feel a little differently about it if the sleeping dog gets awakened and the police start a fresh murder investigation," Tressa pointed out.

Indie showed a little more concern.

"How much do they know for certain? What exactly did you tell them?"

"I told them enough to try to make them understand how psychotic Lucky was. But, God forbid, if I had to deny it in a court of law, the DA wouldn't be able to convict me without a whole lot more." Tressa couldn't believe she was actually weighing the possibility of her children testifying against her in court for accessory to the murder of their father.

"It won't get that far," Indie said with more confidence than she thought he should have. "You're jumping to conclusions."

"How can you be so sure?" she asked.

Indie took a moment. "Because," he said, "if I were them I wouldn't want the police involved."

For a split second Tressa wanted Indie to be right. "Why wouldn't you go to the police?" she asked. "And why do you think their actions would mirror yours?"

"I've been the only father figure they've had for the past ten years, more than half their lives. Those two are more like me than they even know or would want to admit. And the reason I wouldn't want the police involved is simple."

Tressa glared at him, and when he didn't continue, she asked, "Why is that?"

"If I were them," Indie said, "I would want to kill me."

Tressa's heart dropped.

15

Exhaling

Today was one of those rare occasions when Tressa went in to work extra early and was able to leave early. She went by the salon and got her hair done and was home by noon. Eli had to travel out of town and once he got on that plane, she was free to do whatever her heart desired. This was the first time since the boys had been staying with Betty—Tressa refused to use the words "moved out"—that she was actually happy they were gone. Well, maybe happy was too strong of a word. She'd been calling Betty all day, every day, checking on them. But she was definitely grateful for the peace and quiet of the empty house. Work had been maddening and Tressa had no idea how much longer she would be able to keep Eli's illicit secret away from his wife.

But right now all she wanted to do was take a long, hot, relaxing bath. *Thank* God *it was Friday,* she thought. No work until Monday.

She ran the water as hot as she could stand it, dumped in two scoops of lavender bubble salt, and disrobed from her work clothes: crisp white Anne Fontaine blouse, black pencil skirt,

black lace matching La Perla bra and thong, leaving a puddle
of designer garments on the floor. She examined her body in the
full-length mirror affixed to the bathroom door. She squeezed
her breasts, checking their firmness. Her boobs still stood at attention just the way they did when she was eighteen. Wow! She
didn't even want to think about how long ago that was. She was
going to be thirty-five this year, which was the same age that
her mother was when she was found alone and dead in a prison
cell.

After the water was ready Tressa submerged her body, along
with her thoughts of the past and the future, into the oversized
sunken jet-powered tub. "Ahhh," she sighed; the temperature
was perfect.

She loved taking baths with Indie and wished that he was
there with her now. Tressa reminisced about the last time she
and Indie were together and let the tranquil scent of the bubbles
take her away on a Calgon trip.

When she opened her eyes, she was surprised to see Indie
standing over the tub. "Are you just going to stand there and
watch?" she flirted.

"I thought you said you were tired," Indie said with a mischievous smile carved on his face. He was wearing Sean John
jeans and nothing else. His upper body was perfect: not an
ounce of fat.

"Yeah . . ." Tressa said. "Tired, not dead." He was making
her work for it, but like her mother used to say, "If it's not
worth working for it's not worth having." "I'm not the only one
it seems that wants to play." Tressa looked at his crotch and
moistened her lips with her tongue. "Are you going to let your
little Indian come out to play with its squaw or are you going to

keep it locked up in its tent all day?" she asked Indie with a naughty grin.

Indie's russet skin color flushed even more red. "Busted," he said before taking off his jeans. "Make room for me, baby."

And no matter how much room in the tub she made, Indie managed to fill it up with his hands, mouth, and not-so-little Indian!

He started calling her name. "Tressa . . ."

Hearing him chant her name in utter joy turned her on even more. She already was matching his rhythm grind for grind. Tressa was on the brink of a mind-blowing climax. Almost. It was coming. Almost home.

Indie said, "I got a surprise for you, baby."

And Tressa couldn't wait for him to give it to her, but before she could reach that peak she opened her eyes.

Indie stood next to her, fully dressed. She had been day-dreaming. "You gon' drown yourself in that tub," he said. "You want to know what the surprise is?"

Tressa blushed. She was caught with her hand in the cookie jar. The fantasy had to be real. "What's the surprise?"

"This." He held up a brown envelope. "Two tickets to A.C., first-class airline, and first-class hotel suite."

"I thought you had to work this weekend?" Tressa said. He was supposed to fly to Connecticut to check on some property.

"I do," Indie said. "That's why I bought the tickets for you and Missy. I didn't want to leave you at home alone just because I have to work."

Tressa said, "I could've gone with you, honey."

"Yep, you could have. To drive around all day looking at rundown real estate. Or"—he held the tickets up again—"you could spend the weekend in Atlantic City, at a five-star hotel, lounging by the pool, engaging in girl talk during the day and playing a little blackjack at night. Your choice. Especially with everything going on, you could use a break."

"What time does my flight leave?"

"Not until tonight."

"Good," Tressa said. "Then get undressed. You are not the only one in this house with a surprise! Guess what I just found out?" Light danced in his eyes. "I'm pregnant!"

Indie was ecstatic. He didn't have any biological children of his of own. Her news had definitely trumped his!

16

It's a Wrap

Operating out of the renovated storefront on First and Broad Street, It's a Wrap Salon was not only in a prime location, they did the best black hair in the city. At least that's what all of their flyers advertised, and all of its customers agreed. Gypsy, the owner of the shop, didn't hire any stylists that didn't have at least five years of experience under her belt and could fix hair. There was no half steppers there when it came to fixing hair. The clientele were mostly the girlfriends of drug dealers, but no one—regardless of how much dope their boyfriend sold—was seen without an appointment. No walk-ins allowed.

Beside its up-to-date dos, It's a Wrap was also known as the place to catch up on the gossip.

Gypsy was talking to another one of her clients, "You can get your hair done like my client Tressa. I did her hair this morning and it came out looking like a million bucks." Gypsy showed the picture of Tressa to her client in her chair.

"I heard that bitch was getting married this month," Nosey Rosey announced. She got her hair done at It's a Wrap once a month, and she always stirred something up when she visited.

"Tressa who?" someone asked.

"Shawsdale," Nosey Rosey said in a tone that implied: Bitch, don't you know anything? She continued. "The bitch that work for the mayor and thinks she's all that."

"Rosey, if you keep moving your neck like that you're going to make me burn you," her stylist told her.

Dutchess, who was getting her wrap redone, was two chairs down from Nosey Rosey, and at the mention of Tressa's name, her ears perked up.

"Is that the same girl that used to fuck with that crazy-ass nigga named Lucky that had all the money?" another girl asked. "I heard that nigga had like twenty million dollars back in the day, and she up and left him, no backup plan or nothing. And they claim he was the crazy one."

"Tell me about," Nosey Rosey said, pleased that the dumb chick had finally caught on to who she was talking about. "I heard she was getting married to an Indian dude."

"He got money?" the girl asked. Her boyfriend did stickups; her man was always looking for a new lick.

"I don't think that bitch fuck with no broke niggas, that's for sure."

Dutchess listened quietly, wanting to say something to defend Tressa, but she didn't. Instead, she couldn't help reflecting back when Tressa almost set her on fire.

When Tressa found out that Lucky had a bitch living in her old apartment, the one where Tressa lived before Lucky moved her into the mini mansion, saying Tressa flipped the hell out would be an understatement.

"I know you in there, bitch," Tressa had screamed through the door. "You might as well face me like a woman."

Dutchess reflected on how she had almost shit her panties. Up until that moment, screwing Lucky had been all fun and games. Lucky was looking out for her, giving her a little money here and there, and she was hitting him off with pussy anytime he wanted it. Hell, the way Dutchess looked at it, she was far from the only chick Lucky was messing around on Tressa with. But there was no way on *God*'s green earth that Dutchess was going to open that door and face her best friend.

And looking back, she didn't believe it when Tressa threatened to set the place on fire. If Lucky wouldn't have called and told Tressa to leave before the police and fire department arrived, Tressa would have gone to jail. However when Tressa found out that Dutchess was inside, she had torched the friendship. Removing herself from the situation, Dutchess could never blame her.

"Yeah, that bitch need to be checking on her boys instead of worrying bout a nigga," Rosey said.

But Dutchess's mind was still on Tressa and all the good times they had before she double-crossed her best friend. She wondered if Tressa would ever be able to forgive her. She wanted and needed to get back in Tressa's life.

17

Chill-Laxing

After reaching Atlantic City so late, Tressa and Missy decided to hit the sack. Before noon the next day, the girls had already had breakfast and were poolside, catching the last bit of sunrays that summer had to offer.

Tressa wore a stunning white Marc Jacobs two-piece bathing suit. "I'm glad we came," she said.

The cool breeze coming in off of the Atlantic Ocean was blowing through her hair. She hadn't felt this relaxed in months.

"Girl, I don't know how I'm going to repay you for all this," Missy said, her white, high-cut one-piece showing off all her curves.

Tressa had called her at pretty much the last minute and asked if she was busy. After learning about the trip, Missy said she could be ready in forty-five minutes. Before Tressa knew it, Missy was on the porch ringing the doorbell, suitcase in hand, in less than an hour.

"Don't thank me," Tressa said. "I told you Indie set it up. He said with the wedding right around the corner I needed a moment to get away from all the planning, work, and everything else." Tressa left out all the stress she was going through with the twins. Her and Missy were close, but everything wasn't everybody's business. At this point she didn't want to share with her about the baby because she was still in her first trimester.

Missy took a sip from the glass of lemonade that had just been refreshed by the cabana hostess. "Indie's a good man. I've never stayed in a hotel this nice before. Isn't this the same one you and Dutchess used to come to?"

Tressa almost cringed when she heard that name. She and Dutchess used to be best friends. Until Dutchess decided to go behind her back her and fuck Lucky. Tressa was well aware that her baby daddy was a dog, but Tressa never in a million years expected her best friend to break the first cardinal rule of friendship: boyfriends and girlfriends are off limits. To make light of the situation, she chalked it up to Dutchess's belief that BFF stood for Best Fucking Floozy.

"Yeah. We stayed here a few times," Tressa said nonchalantly.

Missy must've caught the not-so-subtle hint because she switched gears. "Where are you and Indie going for your honeymoon?"

The mention of her honeymoon put a smile on Tressa's face. "We haven't completely made up our minds yet," she said. "But it's definitely going to be one of the islands in the Pacific Ocean. Maybe Hawaii or Fiji."

Missy looked like she was trying to visualize a map in her head. "Hawaii's so beautiful," she said after a beat.

"When were you in Hawaii?" Tressa asked skeptically.

"I don't have to go to a place to know that it's gorgeous," Missy said. "And besides, I watch *Hawaii Five-O* on television."

They both laughed. Missy was easy to be with; she didn't front like she was something that she wasn't, and she didn't hate on people because they may have had something that she didn't. That was one of the reasons Tressa chose Missy to be maid of honor.

Missy stopped laughing first. "Can I ask you a serious question?"

Tressa was conscious of the levity of Missy's normally jovial tone.

"I hope I can answer it," she said.

"How do you know when you've really found the right person? I mean, you know, the person you want to spend the rest of your life with?"

"Oh, that's easy." Tressa sat up in her chair to look in Missy's eyes. "When someone loves another person for all the things they do right, they have something." She stirred the ice around in her Pepsi with a straw, then took a sip. "But when you love someone in spite of the things they do wrong, that's when you have something special."

"So what you and Indie share is something special for sure," Missy said.

Tressa smiled. "As special as getting a white pony on your sixteenth birthday," she said.

Missy's forehead wrinkled. "You never told me you had a pony when you were young."

"That's because I didn't," she said, "but you're not the only one that watches television."

They shared another laugh. *Enjoy it while you can,* Tressa told herself. *The weekend will be over before you know it.* Then they both kicked back and enjoyed the time luxuriating. Missy read a book by Nikki Turner and Tressa leafed through a magazine.

Tressa raised her eyes from the tabloid magazines when Beyoncé's "Single Ladies" started blaring from Tressa's cell phone.

She sucked her teeth to express her displeasure of being disturbed from her moment of tranquility. "Who could that be?" she mumbled while begrudgingly searching her bag for the ever-present electronic device. "Here it is." Once she viewed the caller ID she smiled again. "Look a here," she said to Missy, pushing on the button to accept the call. "Hey stranger, long time no hear."

She hadn't spoken to Taj in three months. The last time she heard from him he was in Vegas, the time before that, Miami.

"Don't act like that, sis." She could hear the smile in his voice. "I've been meaning to call you, but you know how it is."

It was a lame excuse but Tressa would forgive him. That's what brothers and sisters did. Missy mouthed, "Who is it?" Tressa didn't pay her any mind. "Whatever," she teased. "So where are you these days?"

"If I told you I'd have to kill you," Taj joked. He never did have a very good sense of humor.

Tressa shot back, "If your ass don't make it to my wedding I'mma kill your stinky-feet butt." He hated it when she talked about his feet. When they were young Taj's feet used to smell so bad their mother would have to keep his sneakers on the porch in order not to funk up the house.

"My dogs don't bark no more, so you can kill that noise," he said. "And you know damn well I ain't fittin' to miss my baby sister's I-dos."

Missy finally figured out who was on the phone. "Let me speak to Taj," she mouthed. She had a crush on Taj, and he liked her too, but Missy had never given him the goodies. Not yet.

Tressa threw up her hands to tell Missy to hold on, and kept talking. "Seriously though," she said to Taj, "how are you doing?" She always worried about him.

Taj stayed away from Richmond for long stretches because the RPD had him on the suspect list for a few open investigations, although they didn't have enough evidence to bring formal charges. The crazy part was that Taj had nothing to do with most of what he was suspected. Nevertheless, Taj was a firm believer in "out of sight, out of mind."

"Everything's beautiful with me, sis. I'm just laying low, spending paper, and having a ball, making up for all that time I spent locked up in that prison cell."

Tressa understood. When Taj was locked up it was tough on both of them. She hated seeing him in prison. "I know that's right," she said, "but you better be spending some of that money on a super-nice wedding gift for me and Indie."

"Stop playing, girl. You know I gotcha. Have I ever not come through for you? And I always will," he added before she could answer.

Missy pouted, eyeing Tressa with an annoyed expression.

"Missy say to tell you hi." Tressa eyed her back. "Satisfied?" she asked Missy.

"Oh, yeah," Taj exclaimed. "Ask her when she's going to give me those drawers to sniff on?"

"You nasty, boy." Tressa turned her nose up like there was an odor wafting through the air. "Ask her yourself." When she handed the phone to Missy, the pout her friend was sporting seconds earlier flipped into a smile.

18

The Blood

Soft, yellow slivers of light from the street lamp sliced through the closed blinds of the window, casting elongated shadows on the east-facing wall, providing the only light in Betty's bedroom.

Tick . . . tick . . . tick . . . tick . . .

The only sound in the room came from the old wind-up clock, which was loud enough to wake the dead, sitting on the night table alongside the queen-sized bed. The fluorescent-green hands indicated the time was 12:45 A.M. Betty was normally sound asleep by ten o'clock every night but the never-ending ticking sound wasn't the reason she was still awake. She'd been unable to sleep ever since Hadji and Ali had moved in with the story of their mother and stepdad possibly being responsible for her son's death.

She looked to the scriptures for guidance.

Betty, a God-fearing woman, trusted her faith. And to believe in God, it was only natural to believe in the devil. She once heard that "the greatest trick the devil ever pulled was to convince the world that he didn't exist." But Betty wasn't fooled by

Satan's deceiving shenanigans because she had met him in his physical form. The corporal being the devil had used to reveal himself to Betty was Khalil "Lucky" Foster, her own son.

Betty first noticed that Khalil was evil when he was only seven years old. He wasn't like the other children his age; Khalil's pranks always involved torture of some sort. He cherished inflicting pain, emotional or physical, on people or animals, and watching his victims suffer.

One time Betty went into the backyard to hang clothes on the clothesline and noticed red blotches all over the lawn. It resembled blood, which startled her. She had no idea where it came from. Then she remembered that Khalil was supposed to have mowed the grass earlier that morning while she was at work.

Then she really started to panic. "Oh, my God!" she prayed out loud, hoping her son hadn't hurt himself. She rushed back inside the house to Khalil's room to make sure he was okay.

When Betty walked into her son's room, she found Khalil lying on the bed reading a comic book. *Thank you, Lord!* He didn't seem to be hurt. Relieved, but still confused, Betty asked, "Where did all the blood in the backyard come from?"

"What blood?" Khalil didn't even bother to pull his eyes away from the magazine. "I didn't see any blood," he said nonchalantly.

How could he have missed it? Betty thought. The yard was literally painted crimson. "Khalil, the backyard is covered with blood. Are you saying it wasn't that way when you cut the grass this morning?"

Khalil answered with a single word: "Nope," and he continued to browse the comic. He acted as if he wasn't remotely interested in what she was talking about.

The fact that Khalil was so casual about the situation aroused Betty's curiosity even more. And she was determined to get to the bottom of it; she knew where to look for answers.

Betty went over to ask her neighbor Mrs. Prichard if she had seen anything unusual. It was a known fact that Mrs. Prichard lived in the windows of her home, watching everything that went on in the neighborhood. If there was something to be seen, Mrs. Prichard would know.

Betty stepped on Mrs. Prichard's front porch, and the door swung open before Betty could get a chance to knock.

Betty greeted her nosy neighbor cheerfully. "How're you doing today, Mrs. Prichard?" The two had lived beside each other for ten years but they weren't what Betty would call *good friends*. Mrs. Prichard was somewhat of a recluse.

"I'm doing," Mrs. Prichard answered cryptically.

She seemed even more reserved than normal, Betty observed. "Well, uh, if you're not too busy I'd like to have a quick chat with you. I promise not to take up too much of your time."

Mrs. Prichard stared at Betty guardedly, but after a brief hesitation she conceded. "Sure. Come on in."

Once inside, Mrs. Prichard offered Betty a seat. The house was very well maintained, but all the furniture was outdated and covered with thick preserving plastic.

Betty didn't waste any time getting to the matter. "Mrs. Prichard, would you by any chance have seen how all the blood managed to make its way into my backyard? I'm only asking because I know you like to keep an eye on the riffraff."

Her neighbor raised an eyebrow at the question. The gesture made Betty feel that Mrs. Prichard had seen something. "I would appreciate anything you can tell me," Betty added, encouraging Mrs. Prichard to speak up if she knew something.

"Did you ask Khalil?"

Mrs. Prichard's question, in response to her own, caught Betty off guard.

"I did," Betty admitted, "but he doesn't seem to know anything . . . at least that's the way he's acting."

There went the raised brow again.

"That's peculiar," Mrs. Prichard said.

"Why would you say that?" Betty was getting a little frustrated with the baffling responses she was receiving. It was obvious that Mrs. Prichard knew something; it was written all over her face.

"Normally I wouldn't have come to you like this," Betty said. "But all the blood everywhere . . . it's really bothering me. Did someone get shot?"

"It's not human blood," Mrs. Prichard said with the confidence of a person that had witnessed the incident.

"Then what type of blood is it?"

"It's cat blood."

Betty repeated, "*Cat blood?*" Well at least they were getting somewhere. "Do you know how the cat blood got all over my yard?" Betty asked.

"I do."

There goes the bullshit again. Betty wanted to punch Mrs. Prichard right in her raggedy-toothed mouth. Instead, she composed herself and made a silent prayer. *God, please forgive me for my un-Christian-like thoughts.* After a deep breath she tried again. "Can you please tell me what you know?"

Be careful what you ask for.

Mrs. Prichard went on to tell Betty how Khalil had buried at least ten cats in the ground, "Up to their heads," she said. She told her how the poor animals' heads protruded from the surface like some type of weird furry plant. Then she described, in detail, the harrowing cries the cats made as Khalil ran over the defenseless little animals—one by one—with the lawn mower.

The visuals of what had happened ran through Betty's mind and almost made her vomit.

Then Mrs. Prichard confided in Betty, "This wasn't the first time that I've seen Khalil do something like that." She ignored the fact that Betty was turning green from the disgust and disappointment. "But this was the worst yet."

Now Betty sat in her dark room rubbing the crucifix she wore around her neck with her index and middle finger, thinking about Tressa. Was she carrying around this heavy burden all of this time?

If Tressa was in any way responsible for Lucky's death, she had to have a damn good reason: Betty thought Tressa was a good girl. And if she had anything to do with Lucky dying, surely he must have put her in a life-or-death position. Lucky would have left her no other choice.

Betty thought long and hard. "This is all my fault," she said out loud.

If only I had got Khalil the counseling he needed when he was young. Back then she didn't want to admit to the world that her only son was defective.

Betty licked her parched lips. All the reminiscing had made her thirsty. She decided to get a glass of water and check on the twins. The headboard bumped the wall when she rose from the bed. She hoped the noise didn't awaken the boys. After sliding into her housecoat and slippers Betty made her way down the hall, trying to make as little noise as possible. There was no need to wake them just because she couldn't sleep. The door to the guest room where Ali and Hadji slept was closed. Betty eased it open to look inside to check on the boys.

"Well, I'll be damned," Betty cursed. The beds were empty.

19

Do or Die

In the city's West End part of town, the after-hours spot on Rosewood Avenue was packed. Outside, dope boys' cars were lined up bumper to bumper down the block. Inside, those same hustlers were betting stacks of c-notes at a clip, while women sat back, observing the action, sipping mixed drinks, and hoping to be chosen later by one of the winners to party privately.

The heat generated by all the bodies in the craps room was hard to ignore. The air conditioner may as well have not been on, but Ali and Hadji didn't even notice the sticky temperature. They were having a ball watching their mentor do his thing.

Ace shook a closed fist back and forth three times. "Make fo'dice and turn these broke-ass niggaz into believers," he said, before opening his grip and letting the chucks fly out. The dice hit the table and careened off the side rail, spinning and rolling. One landed on deuce while the other kept spinning on one of its corners.

Four was one of the hardest numbers to make when playing craps because it could show up only two ways: two-two or three-one. Right now if the remaining live die landed on deuce Ace would win, but if it landed on five he would lose. Everyone in the room collectively held their breath, awaiting the outcome of the roll; most had either bet against the point or just hated on Ace for being so damn lucky.

The second die pirouetted like a professional ice-skater on a sheet of smooth ice; it felt like it would never stop. But it finally did.

Unbelievable.

A deuce, which sucked the remaining air clean out of the room.

Ace smirked in victory. "There he go," he chanted while raking in a pile of money. "My main man, lil' Joe. I told y'all niggaz I was going to make you believers, didn't I?" This was the sixth straight point Ace had made and he had bet heavily on them all. Most of the dudes in the room weren't feeling his good fortune.

Ace and the twins were the only ones smiling.

Laylo was born and raised in the West End and not only was he Ace's competition, he owned the club. "You act like that's the first time you ever won any money, nigga. You still gambling or you fittin' to run and take that little bit of change back across town with you?" There was no love lost between the two hustlers. But even though Laylo and Ace had never really gotten along, for the most part they respected each other.

"Don't let your feelings get your bankroll all fucked up," Ace said, welcoming the challenge. "I just came to socialize, wet my beak, and show my little homies a good time. But I ain't ever been scurred to win no bread, my nigga. Shoot twenty-five hundred." Ace dropped two and a half stacks on the table to show he was dead serious.

Cats looked at Laylo like Ace was trying to punk him. Laylo, feeling the pressure, called the bet.

"Be careful what you ask for," Ace said as the dice took flight from his palm. This time they landed on six-four.

Ten was the second hardest number to point.

"Can't make it this money." Laylo dropped ten G's on the table. "Show me where your heart at."

Ace called the bet without a second thought. "Anybody else got some they trying to give away?" He was in the zone. And "scared money couldn't make money" was his mantra.

A few more cats dropped money on the faded burgundy felt-top table. Ace didn't even bother to ask how much was in the small stacks. Because in his eyes it simply didn't make a difference. He called the bets, grabbed the dice from the table, rattled them against each other in his closed palm, and then spoke to them. "Daddy got enough money to buy shoes for the whole hood, but it's time to get a new Benz," he said. "Show yourself, big-boy Benz." The chucks were in the air before Ace finished his spiel. They tumbled all the way to the far end of the table.

"Six-two."

There were no bets on eight; all the money was on ten for which Ace win and seven for which the house would win. He rolled the red-and-black dice four more times: six-three, three-two, five-one, and four-two.

No winners.

"I tell you what," Ace said to no one in particular. "I got two thousand to one that the dice make *ten or four* before they show seven."

"I'll take that bet twice." It was Dirty Red. "You sweet as molasses."

Ace peeled off another four G's, dropping the cash on the table. "Nothing but a word," he boasted. "Anybody else?"

No takers.

Ace went through the motions and shot the dice again. There was at least thirty-five thousand scattered on the table in various piles. More money than the average blue-collar worker made in a year. Blood money, drug money, ill-gotten money, stolen money . . . nobody gave a damn what it was called—just don't call it counterfeit.

The anticipation that filled the room rose with every shot. No one breathed until the dice came to a halt. But this time when the chucks finally stopped rolling both cubes showed *fives.*

"Fuck!" Dirty Red wasn't too happy about the outcome.

Laylo picked up the dice and threw them across the room. They bounced off the wall. If it wasn't his house, and his dice, he probably would've accused Ace of cheating. "I see you got a horseshoe up your ass tonight, huh?" Laylo's face was so tight he could barely squeeze the words past his big purple lips.

Hadji and Ali looked at Ace; he didn't appear to be the least bit fazed by Laylo's insult. "I'm not a fan of putting anything in my ass," Ace said with a smile. "I guess my freaky isn't quite as freaky as yours. You got me beat there."

A couple cats snickered. Laylo seemed to take the remark for what it was: just a little shit talking. But the shit was a lot harder to swallow after losing twenty stacks.

Ace was nobody's fool. He could feel the tension thicken in the room. "Drinks on me," he said in an attempt to lighten the mood.

Dirty Red took Ace up on his offer. "I'll take a double of

Hen." He would have to sell crack all day to get the money back he lost.

A few more gamblers made orders. Laylo wasn't one of them. Ace told a runner to let the bartender know that all the drinks were on him for the next thirty minutes. "I'm in a good mood tonight," he said.

For the next hour chicks were trying to attract Ace's interest, but his mind wasn't on pussy. He got Ali and Hadji's attention. "I hate to break up all the fun, but it's time for us to get out of here," Ace told the boys.

Ali and Hadji were sitting back enjoying the attention being bestowed upon them by the older women. Most of the girls thought the twins were just "too cute" and couldn't keep their hands off the boys.

Ace scanned his surroundings. The same way he'd been doing the whole time. The aura in the club was off-kilter. He could feel the change in the air. This was a talent he'd picked up from the streets and doing time, where attitudes could change at a moment's notice—and often times no notice at all. Earlier, after putting a major dent in the craps game, he was faced with a spur-of-the-moment judgment call: leave the club immediately (and maybe come off a little scared), or hang around and take a stab at relieving the sudden hostility by tossing a few G's around.

Ace knew now that he'd made a huge mistake. By waiting, he'd given cats a chance to manifest their scheming thoughts into an actuality. He was on the wrong side of town—the city was much more territorial than it was in the nineties—with enough cash to choke a goat. What was he thinking? Ace tried to act casual, like he wasn't up on game, and he whispered to the twins,

"I need y'all to go to the bathroom and make sure your guns are cocked and off safety."

"What's going on?" Although Ali was the one who asked, Ace could see the question floating around in Hadji's eyes as well.

"It could be nothing," Ace said, "but I'm not going to make the mistake of treating it as such. We may have to bang our way up out of here." At least Ace had had enough sense not to drink while he was there. His mind was clear. "Hopefully I'll be able to read the situation before it goes down, if it goes down at all, and I'll tell you what to do in advance. Now, go take care of what I asked you to do and I'll put you up on the rest when you come back."

Ali and Hadji were gone for less than three minutes. They returned ready. Any man confronting the possibility of being hurt by another harbored a certain degree of fear. What separated the champ (or G) from the chump was how he reacted to the fear. The chump ran away from the confrontation and the champ ran toward it. He faced it head on. The twins also had the arrogance of youth on their side: they felt invincible.

It was a good thing Ace had the foresight to have taken them to the shooting range earlier. Practice makes perfect. And the boys had taken to the pistols like a diabetic to sugar. But that was practice; no one was shooting back. "Remember what I taught you today," Ace said. "If it comes down to it, point and shoot. It's as simple as that. You both got two clips, right?" The twins nodded. "That's thirty-two shots each. Way more than you'll need, but don't waste bullets." If the twins were anything like their father, Ace knew what the answer to his next question would be. "Y'all ready?"

Ali said, "Yeah."

"We've been ready," Hadji said. "You the one doing all the talking."

"True that," Ace said. "Just stay by me and follow your instincts. When your gut doesn't tell you what you need to know, I will. Now let's get the fuck out of here."

Ace smiled at a few chicks, but he was really observing cats' actions and body language—both the men and women—as he and the twins made their way to the front door. Any edge he could gain would be a plus. He saw a dude wearing jean shorts make a phone call. He spoke for a few seconds then hung up. Maybe he was alerting someone of their departure. Maybe not.

The bouncer said, "You leaving already, Ace?" He was six-four and cock diesel.

Ace knew he had been locked down with the dude at one of the major prisons, but he couldn't place the name. If his memory was on point, dude used to spend half his time on the weight pile and the other chasing punks. Then he remembered what they used to say about prison faggots: suck dick, tell lies, and keep something going.

"Yeah, I'm out, unless you know a reason we should stay?"

"I-I was just making small talk, Ace." Ace didn't miss the nervous stammer. "You call all the shots," the bouncer finished.

Ace locked eyes with him so that there would be no misunderstanding. "You better believe I do. I know when I'm being fucked too. Nor do I forget who's with me or against me." Ace wasn't sure which had gotten bigger: the dude's eyes or the lump in his throat.

"Man, I ain't got nothing to do with this shit. It's Laylo."

The shot in the dark paid off. Ace asked, "How many?"

"All I know is that Laylo called two of his boys. Said if you thought you were going to come in his spot, disrespect him, and leave with more than a hundred thou you must be crazier than you look. Vince and Johnny's waiting for you to go to your car. I swear man, that's all I know."

"Don't sweat it, dude. I believe you." Ace slipped three hundred-dollar bills in the bouncer's hand. "Thanks for the info."

Ace stepped out of the club with Ali and Hadji by his side. A few people were standing around jawboning, but Ace didn't see Vince or Johnny anywhere. "Be on point," he told the boys. "I'm not sure if they gon' try their hand on the route or once we get to the car."

"Is that you, Ace?"

The lady—smooth chocolate skin, long hair, eyes and teeth bright enough to light the night—stepped out of a green Camry.

Ace eyed her skeptically. Never can be too careful. *This wouldn't be the first time, nor the last, that a beautiful hot chick was used to set a nigga up,* he thought.

"It's me—Dutchess," she said.

"Oh, shit," he said, still on alert, "the last time I seen you, you had short hair."

"Yeah, that was about eight years ago. And you were a lot thinner then," she reminded him.

"Touché," he said. "It was good to see you, but we're kinda in a hurry."

Dutchess gestured with her eyes toward the twins. "Are these your sons?"

"Naw—these are Lucky's boys," he said casually. "It was nice seeing you though."

Dutchess stood and watched as they walked off. But *these are Lucky's boys* continued to ring in her head.

Ace's truck was parked around the corner because he didn't want to advertise that he was inside the club. He removed the Glock from underneath his shirt and jacked the slide. A .45 caliber hollow point jumped in the chamber.

"But we gon' be ready, either way," he said.

The twins followed his lead and took their guns out, cocked and ready.

The few people that were outside paid them no mind. It wasn't uncommon to walk to and from an after-hours spot toting heat. But when they bent the corner, Ace felt something was out of place. One of those big green super cans the city passed out for trash sat by his truck. It wasn't there earlier. He noticed the bushes in front of the house that his Escalade was parked in front of cast shadows up against the bricks that were the wrong shape.

These clowns had made it easy. He whispered to the boys, "The trash can." They saw it. "I want both of you to dump three shots apiece in it when I say so. I'll take care of the rest."

The twins nodded. They were ready. Hadji's eyes couldn't hide his excitement. He wanted to be just like his daddy. And if his daddy was a killer, then that's what he wanted to be. Ali was equally as pumped up, however, for different reasons. It didn't matter why or how he'd gotten into this situation. He knew that if they didn't do it right the first time, they may not live to see their next birthday.

Ace gave them one last look. "Now!" he said.

Pop. Pop. Pop. Pop . . .

The thunder from the twins' guns going off brought Johnny

from behind the bush like a Jack-in-the-box, and that's exactly what Ace hoped would happen.

Ace double-tapped the trigger of his own pistol: *Phut! Phut!*

The silencer muted the sound, like the door closing on a Mercedes-Benz. But the impact snatched Johnny from his feet, throwing him into the brick wall of the house—the same wall that had exposed his shadow—before his limp body crashed to the ground. The high-velocity exploding bullets had shattered his breast plate, making it appear as if an angry waitress had flung an oversized bowl of spaghetti sauce all over his upper body, cooking his innards.

Ace heard that the final two shots were fired by the twins. All six of theirs hit its target as well. Ace had heard a grunt when the first slug pierced the plastic receptacle. There was no need to look inside. Vince and Johnny could convene later wherever it was that dead G's ended up to discuss what went wrong.

A half an hour had passed since they had made their getaway, when in the SUV Ace turned the volume on the sound system all the way down. The twins could hear their heartbeats drum inside their chests. Ace casually maneuvered the truck through the sparsely populated streets like nothing unusual had taken place.

"You did good back there," he said, keeping his eyes in front of him on the road. The SUV stopped at a red light on Belvedere and Broad. "You okay?" This time he was looking at them, first at Hadji and then Ali.

"No doubt," Hadji boasted. He was an adrenaline junkie. Later in life he would probably have to race motorcycles or participate in some other extreme sports to quench that insatiable thirst. "I'm cool." But that wasn't totally the truth.

Ace craned his head around so that he could see in the backseat. "How about you, Ali? You cool too?"

Ali felt a lot of things right at that moment, but cool wasn't one of them. In fact, he was hot. His heart felt like the engine of a race car. "Yeah, I'm cool," he lied.

"Good," Ace said. "Cool is good. You know you can't talk to anyone about what happened tonight, right? No one but me," he specified. "This has to be kept one hundred percent between us, ya dig?"

No one said anything. The light turned green.

The twins felt Ace's eyes on them before taking off. "Nobody," he said once again.

20

Busted

After the fatal incident of the two stick-up men at the club, the boys were finally back at Betty's house and out of harm's way.

It was 2:30 in the morning when the twins put their feet on their grandmother's porch. The lights were still out, just like before they had left. Ali dug into his pocket for the key she'd given them. After retrieving it, he eased it into the key slot. The door opened with a squeak.

"Be quiet," Hadji whispered. "You gon' get us caught." Like he was the only one not trying to get tore off.

After everything they had been through tonight, the last thing they needed was to be interrogated by their grandma.

Ali whispered back, "What do you think I'm trying to do?"

They slipped inside. With both hands, Ali gently closed the door and reset the deadbolt. "We made it," he said, exhaling. And right when they thought they were out of the woods, the lights flashed on.

There was no doubt they were busted.

Betty sat in her recliner, hair all rolled up in hard pink hair rollers, wearing a flowery patterned housecoat and slippers, with a cup of coffee sitting on the end table beside her. Although she didn't raise her voice, there was no mistaking her anger.

"What in the devil are you two doing sneaking in and out of my house like little heathens?"

Ali and Hadji eyeballed each other, mentally pulling straws, to decide who would speak up first. Ali drew the short end. "We are not sneaking, Grandma . . ." He was trying to come up with an explanation. "We just got hot and couldn't sleep." The house's central-air unit wasn't kicking the cold air it used to and Betty had someone scheduled to come out the next day to take a look at it. It was a plausible excuse.

Hadji was nodding in agreement, looking like a bobble-head doll on the dashboard of an old car.

"So," Ali continued, "we just went outside to get some air."

Betty looked as if she was processing what Ali had told her. "Outside where?" she asked. "And don't say Johnny's because I already called his mother. He's in bed—where you should be."

Ali was glad Betty had exposed her hand before he made the mistake of saying he was with Tommy. "We were out back at the rec."

"At the rec, huh?" Betty didn't sound as if she were buying it.

"Yeah," Hadji said.

Ali was glad Hadji had finally decided to help out.

"We were shooting basketball." Hadji realized his mistake as soon as it rolled off his tongue.

"Then where is the ball?" Betty asked, looking around. "You didn't come in with one."

Think fast! Think fast! Think fast! "We were shadow shooting," Hadji said.

What the hell is shadow shooting? Ali thought. *Hadji going to get us in more trouble than we already are.*

Betty crinkled her face like she could smell the lie. "What is shadow shooting?"

Ali couldn't wait to hear this one himself.

Hadji came through. "It's when you go through the motions of a shot, but without the ball," he said.

"It's called muscle memory recognition," Ali added.

"That's how Kobe Bryant got so good," Hadji finished.

"Well, Kobe Bryant ain't staying with me and I don't give a damn about no muscle memories or muscle Alzheimer's for that matter," Betty preached. "You need to let me know when you want to leave this house. You two scared me half to death. This ain't them suburbs where you and your mother live; it's dangerous out here late at night. You hear me?"

"Yes, ma'am," they said in unison. "We didn't mean to make you upset with us," Ali said to his grandmother in the most sincere tone.

"I'm not upset with you," Betty said. "I just don't want anything to happen to you. I wouldn't be able to live with myself. That's if your mother didn't kill me first."

Hadji said, "Sorry, Grandma."

Ali echoed, "Sorry, Grandma."

And they both kissed her on the cheek.

Betty was back to her grandmotherly protective self.

"Do you mind if we go to our room?" Ali asked. "We're kind of tired now."

"I bet you are tired," Betty said. "You can go, but remember what I told you."

"Yes, ma'am."

When they reached their room, both boys breathed a sigh of a relief. They hadn't lied when they told Betty they were tired. They were exhausted. The night had been crazy. They'd actually killed someone.

"You want to talk about it?" Ali asked.

"Ace said we couldn't," Hadji reminded him.

"He didn't mean to each other. If we can't speak among ourselves then who do we talk to?"

If their dad was alive they could talk to him about what had just happened and how they should feel about it. It definitely wasn't the type of thing a teenager told his mother, and discussing anything with Indie was out of the question.

"We can talk to Ace," Hadji said.

Ali wasn't sure if he trusted Ace as much as Hadji did. "Besides Ace," he said.

Hadji ignored the question, his finger to the wall, pantomiming like it was a gun, and pulled the trigger. *Boom!* "I'm still pumped," he said.

"Me too," Ali admitted. "But how do you feel about it?"

"About what?"

"Killing someone?"

Hadji thought about the question this time and then looked his brother head on. "I think them niggas got what they deserved; that's how I feel. What about you? How do you feel about it?"

Ali was more ambivalent about the situation. "I know for a fact that if we hadn't did what we did we wouldn't be here talking about it. But at the same time, I'm not sure if it was right, bro," he said.

Hadji didn't get it. "That don't make sense," he said. "How

can it be wrong to bust a nigga in the ass that's trying to kill you? If that's wrong, then I don't want to be right."

Ali sighed. "You think I'm sounding soft, don't you?"

"You said it, not me."

"But you know it's not true."

Hadji knew that of the two of them, Ali had more heart. Ali got into the first fight at school, taking up for him. He was the first one to dive off the high board into the deep end of the pool. He was the first one that talked Hadji into playing football with the midget team against the older boys—who liked to hit hard—when they were only peewees. Although they were twins Ali had always taken the role of older brother, even if it was only by eleven seconds.

"All I'm saying is we shouldn't make this kind of thing a habit. We survived this one, but will we be this lucky next time?"

21

In the Trenches

Some of everybody loved Richmond's Mayor Eli Walters: Democrats, Republicans, white people, and especially, the black people. He had a way of making the people feel as though he was one of them. He was one of the most popular mayors since D.C.'s Marion Barry and Rudy Giuliani in New York.

He'd grown up in the projects and joined the Marines to fight for his country while putting himself through college. Eli had been a fighter pilot for the Marines when the United States went into Panama to get Noriega and volunteered for the first Desert Storm campaign. He got into politics so others coming from an underprivileged background, like himself, could have the opportunity to follow in his footsteps and make a better life for themselves. He ran his campaign with the slogan "Eli Will Battle 4 You" and his constituents truly felt like he was fighting for their best interests. But his popularity was sagging slightly due to crime and the economy.

Today Eli was on his way to make an appearance at a cookout smack dead in the middle of Cyprus Court. He held identical events in all of the city's housing developments every year since he was elected, one after the other throughout the summer.

Accompanied by his press secretary, Marvin, Eli rode in the backseat of his city-funded Lincoln, thinking about his future. He told his driver, "Take the long way, Tony. I want a few extra minutes. I have an important phone call to make."

"The police chief has got you stressed, huh?" Marvin asked, already knowing the answer.

Eli only nodded.

"Well, if anything can be done in this city, you're the one to make it happen. And remember, crime has been at its lowest since before you took office."

"I know, but recently it's been rising."

"It's summertime and more people are out when it gets hot."

"You're right, but we gotta get this under control. Re-election is in a few months."

"Well, the people love you, Eli, and they see your progress."

"I appreciate those kind words, Marvin. I truly do."

He and Marvin had been together since they met in college. Marvin was the one who had introduced Eli to Ivy. He was Eli's press secretary, confidant, advisor, and best friend.

Eli scrolled through the directory in his BlackBerry and after finding the number he was looking for, pushed the call button.

The phone rang several times. Normally he would've disconnected after the third ring but it was urgent that he got through.

After the sixth ring, a deep voice rumbled, "Yeah, this is Casino."

Casino was a prominent business owner, a well-respected power player, and an OG. The hood loved Casino even more than they did Eli. If a dime bag of Kush was sold, Casino not only knew about it, he probably got a cut off it. He had that rare trait where people not only respected him but they feared him as well.

"I thought you were going to help me out," Eli said. "If much more blood spills this summer, the city's going to be in an uproar. I have enough to worry about with the economy doing as poor as it is."

"Hold what you got, Eli. I understand that you have problems. Shit, everyone has problems these days." Casino sounded calm and collected, like he was the one in charge. "But I said that I would *try* to help you out. I didn't promise you anything."

Eli knew that Casino was milking the situation for all it was worth. The more Eli depended on him, the more favors Casino would demand later on down the line. They both knew how to play the game.

"Cut the shit, Casino. You don't *try* to do anything. If I wanted somebody to fucking try I would've left the situation in the hands of the RPD," Eli said, feeding Casino's already large ego. "Besides me, you're the most influential figure in Richmond."

Eli imagined that Casino was cheesing it up at the compliment. "You mean I'm the most influential person in this city . . . in spite of you," Casino shot back below the waist.

Eli had to suck it up if he wanted the man's help with getting a handle on the violence. Casino's was the only word that gangbangers would listen to. "If your head gets any bigger it's going to be awfully difficult to find a hat to fit you," Eli half joked. "But I don't have to shop for you so I'll let you deal with that. What I do need"—Eli paused for emphasis—"is to be able to count on you when I need you."

The phone went silent. Eli hoped he hadn't overshot his hand and offended his part-time ally. He needed Casino—for now.

"Don't get your panties in a knot," Casino said. "Have I ever let you down? Just don't forget who you run to when shit gets too hot."

And I've always returned the favor, Eli thought. What started out as a fruitful relationship for both men was starting to feel more like extortion to Eli. Casino's demands of him were becoming more and more outlandish, the relationship was quickly going to shit. "I won't forget you, Casino. You can count on that." Eli ended the call just as his car pulled up to Cyprus Court's recreation center.

Tony came around and opened the car door for him. Eli stepped out among his many supporters. He'd traded in his trademark custom-made suit for a more relaxed outfit of jeans, Gucci loafers, and a button-up shirt with the sleeves rolled up. Homemade signs had been posted on the wall of the building in his honor. Among them:

Eli Will Battle 4 You!!!
I'll Go to War 4 Eli Walter Any Day

Eli beamed and began to shake hands, kiss babies, and fill his stomach, and catered to the people of Cyprus Court with some of that good-smelling barbecue chicken that was simmering on the huge commercial grill.

It was a good day; so much so that Eli didn't even mind that much when Chief Higgins ambushed him. "Have you read the paper?"

Eli read the paper religiously every morning. Not just the *Richmond Times* but *The New York Times* as well. "Yeah," he said, "I browsed through it."

"I thought you said your man could get this under control?" Chief Higgins was about two or three inches shorter than Eli and wasn't in nearly as good shape. Eli worked out daily, the way he did when he was in the military.

Eli wanted to tell him to shut the fuck up since he'd just been on the phone selling his soul to Casino. "I'm on top of it," he said instead. "You do understand, it's not going to happen overnight. Besides, we're only four homicides above where we were last year. It seems like more because most of them have been committed during the summer. People pay more attention in the summer months because the kids are out of school."

"It's also the time when tempers run hot and riots jump off," Chief Higgins pointed out.

Eli saw Tressa's boys near the basketball court and figured this might be a good time to speak to the twins, like he'd promised Tressa, and get out of this conversation. "I need to talk to some fellas, Donald, but you've made your point." Before the chief could protest Eli had already walked off. "Ali, Hadji, how're you guys doing?" He gave each boy a firm handshake.

"We cool, Mayor Walters," Hadji said indifferently.

"What's with the Mayor Walters stuff? Call me Eli. We just chilling, that's all.

"How're things going at the house with your new stepdad?

Your mother mentioned to me that you all aren't completely feeling it yet?"

"We don't have a stepdad," Hadji was the first to say. "My mother isn't married."

Ali rolled his eyes at his brother. "We just had a few misunderstandings, that's all. No big deal."

Eli put a hand on each of their shoulders and spoke to them like they were old fishing buddies. "I know firsthand how difficult it can be letting a man into your life who isn't your father. You're not always going to see eye-to-eye, nor should you. As long as he does right by you and your mother, you should give the guy a chance. He deserves that, doesn't he?"

Ali squeezed out, "Maybe." Hadji mumbled something under his breath that Eli couldn't make out.

"Good enough," Eli said. "How would you like to come by City Hall sometime so we can talk, if I get your mother to bring you? You guys can give me some pointers about how to keep this city of ours afloat. You know, from a teenage perspective."

Hadji wasn't all that excited by the offer, but Ali said sure. That was good enough. Eli gave the boys another pat on the shoulder. "It's a deal then. I'll make the arrangements with your mother."

"You do that," Ali said, impressed, although Hadji seemed far less enthused.

The mayor slipped off into the crowd as the boys' friend Tommy walked up and asked, "We still got plan Shut It Down in motion?"

"I don't think we should," Ali said, hesitating.

"Man, forget that. We ain't spend our money for nothing. We got to." Hadji was always up for being mischevious.

"Everything set up?" Ali asked.

"Yeah, man," Tommy assured Ali.

"Well, everybody take your positions," Ali said.

"Roger that," Hadji said in a walkie-talkie even though Ali and Tommy were both there. As darkness fell, the boys let off the firecrackers, breaking up the party and causing everybody to run for cover. Food flew everywhere, but the funniest part to the boys was seeing Eli's security scramble to get him to the car and out of the hood.

The boys laughed so hard, and Hadji said, "Well, I guess the mayor ain't prepared for battle after all."

22

First and Last Warning

The sun had finally decided to take a break from tormenting the city and in appreciation the basketball courts behind the Cyprus Court recreation center came to life. Things were in full summertime swing. Young Jeezy's latest mix tape knocked from the back of a red Durango with tinted windows and red-and-chrome twenty-four-inch rims. Dudes, mostly shirtless, ran up and down the court with a controlled recklessness. These were the A-league guys showing off for the girls. And a never-ending line of kids waited to be served by the Mr. Softee ice-cream truck. Old man Pop, and his raggedy bootleg truck, was still barred from the projects until he learned not to cheat the little ones.

Most of the crowd watching the game screamed, "Ooohh shit!" all at the same time, in reaction to a rock-the-cradle windmill dunk.

"What happened?" Ali asked, looking up from his iPod a little too late.

"You missed it," Hadji told his brother. Ali was upset he'd

missed it, but maybe somebody caught it on a camera phone, he thought. That was the hood's version of instant replay.

Drawing the spotlight to himself, Ace dug a Franklin from his pocket, dropped it on the ground, and yelled at Tank, "I got a buck you can't do that again." Tank nodded his head like "I gotcha ya."

The next time Tank got the ball and took flight the guy guarding him did the right thing: moved out of the way. In mid-flight, Tank threaded the ball between his legs then cocked it back so far with his left hand it looked like his shoulder blade pop out of its socket. Ali was on top of the action this time. Every set of eyes on the playground was on Tank. He was putting so much force into the slam surely the backboard was going to need to be replaced. And then it happened.

"Ah damn." He missed.

The ball caught the back of the rim and flew fifty feet, landing near the monkey bars. Then the laughter erupted. Somebody screamed, "That dude made a Sprite commercial!"

And the jokes continued until Indie walked up from seemingly out of nowhere and confronted Ace. "I need to see you." His body language suggested that he was making a statement rather than a request.

When the boys caught a glimpse of Indie their eyes swelled to the size of Ping-Pong balls. What was Indie doing in Cyprus Court? Besides trying to get his head peeled back.

Ace sucked in a lungful of air, pushing his chest out. "You see me now. What up?"

Indie hauled off and slapped skin from Ace's face. Ace stumbled back a few steps before reaching for his pistol, but Indie already had a chrome 9mm Glock trained on him. "I wish your pussy ass would," Indie hissed with a steady glare. Ace dropped his hands back by his side. "You got these young cats out here fooled like you a real live gorilla or something." Indie looked at Ace with disgust. "But remember I know your true pedigree."

The park had gone as silent as a graveyard. Everybody wanted to see and hear how the confrontation would unfold. Indie continued to verbally berate Ace. "You's a bitch-ass teddy bear. You were a flunky for Lucky back in the day and now you trying to live off what he did in the past. But when it comes to my boys, this is my first and final warning to you. . . ."

Ali watched Ace's eyes; they were focused on Indie like his life depended on it. And maybe it did.

"If I ever find out you put one of my boys in harm's way again, you going to wish your crackhead mother had sucked your junky daddy off and spit you out instead of fucking him. Now tell me if you understand me?"

Hadji was waiting for Ace to turn up the heat. No way was Ace going to let Indie punk him in his own projects. No way could this happen. Ace was the man in Cyprus Courts.

Blood dripped from Ace's busted lip. It was already beginning to swell. He stammered, "W-whatever you say, Indie, I don't want it with you."

The onlookers couldn't believe what they had heard or witnessed, and the spectacle Indie had made of Ace broke Hadji's young heart. Indie had punked Ace and he wasn't finished.

Indie rubbed more salt in the already gaping wound. "I didn't hear you," he said. "Say it louder."

"I said"—Ace not only repeated himself but actually increased the volume—"I don't want any problems with you, Indie."

194   Nikki Turner

"Like I said before: last and final warning." Then Indie's eyes rested on the twins. "Get in the car." His Porsche Cayenne was parked in front of the rec center.

Ali took heed and headed to the car while Hadji's feet were stuck in place. Although he'd seen it with his own eyes, he didn't want to believe that Ace had let Indie do this to him. He wanted Ace to get up and do something, but sad to say, Ace did nothing.

When Indie pulled the Cayenne around Hadji looked to Ace, shook his head, and got in. His strip daddy had let him down.

Indie drove around the corner to Betty's house. "Look, go ahead in there and get your stuff together. Y'all coming home. Your mother is worried sick about you. You should be ashamed of yourself, hurting your mother like that." Their submissive body language was all the apology Indie needed . . . for now.

23

History Will Not Repeat Itself

Betty was in the kitchen fixing dinner for the boys, and listening to the television news while she cooked. She sat down at the kitchen table to get a better look when she heard the newscaster announce the headline story. She turned the volume up, and glued her eyes to the screen.

The news anchor said, "Two men were found dead in the 9800 block of Rosemount Avenue, a half block away from a known after-hours, illegal gambling house.

"When officers responded to the shots fired at one thirty-five in the morning, two victims were found dead from multiple gunshot wounds. One in a trash can, and the other in the bushes, said Richmond police spokesperson, Travis Jester.

"As of now," the anchor resumed, "there are no suspects or witnesses to the horrific murders. The victims have been identified as thirty-one-year-old Vincent Taylor and twenty-seven-year-old Johnathan Taylor.

"The brothers had extensive criminal records for assault, robbery, and numerous drug convictions. This makes the seventh and eighth murders this month in the city"—the camera panned to the police chief, Donald Higgins—"No, this isn't going to be like it was in the nineties when the murder rate was at an all-time high. We will get this under control," he said.

Back to the news reporter: "Police went door-to-door asking for information and trying to make their presence known. One person, that wishes to remain anonymous, said, 'I was lying in bed asleep when I heard the shots. It scared the shit out of me. We normally don't get that type of thing out here too often, I hope y'all get that mother—'"

There was a *beep* that covered the word up.

"But as of right now the culprit or culprits remain at large, and the gruesome murders, unsolved. If anyone has any information pertaining to this crime or any other crime call the City of Richmond . . . 800-Lock-U-UP.

"Your identity will be kept secret and you may receive up to a ten-thousand-dollar reward."

Betty turned down the television and began praying for those murdered boys' families. Her heart went out to them. Next, she prayed for her grandsons. She begged God not to let them be like their father and that God would protect them and keep them out of danger. Her prayers were shortened when she heard the phone ring. She knew that Tressa was out of town and it might be an emergency—and indeed it was.

"Praise the Lord," Betty answered.

"Betty, really quick, are the boys there?" Tressa's voice sounded frantic.

"No, not right now. They're over at the rec. Is there anything wrong?"

"I'm not sure," Tressa said. "I'm in Atlanta, on business, but I got a call from a girl I used to know. I don't even know how she got my number, but she claims to have seen the boys with this guy that used to hang out with Lucky. Supposedly, they were at the club that's been on the news." Tressa wanted to go into as little detail on the phone as possible.

"Oh, my God! You don't think—" Betty's mind began to run wild. "Oh Lord . . . Father . . . No!" Betty started to talk to God, but Tressa cut her off.

"I'm not sure what's going on, but I know it's not good. I can feel it."

"Oh, Father," Betty said.

"I don't want to say much on this phone, and I'm sure you can read between the lines, but I want you to put those boys on lockdown. Pray, I don't know what else to do."

"Listen, I'm going to have to put my foot down," Betty said, "all the way down and tell these boys myself what I know." Betty shook her head, then she heard a door close outside of her door. "I think that's the boys right there. I will call you back. But between me and my God, we got this." Betty tried to assure Tressa before hanging up the phone.

As Betty made her strides to meet the boys at the door, she talked to God, "Oh, Savior Jesus Christ, please Lord, give me the strength."

Betty couldn't act like she didn't see what was going on any longer. Ali and Hadji were following in their father's footsteps more and more everyday. She could see it in the way they talked, the way they wore their clothes, the expressions and gestures they made when they thought no one was looking. Betty had made a vow to herself: she would be a better grandparent to the twins than she was a mother to their father. If she ignored what was right in front of her eyes and let those young boys go wayward, she wouldn't be honoring that promise she made to her son that went along with the videos that he made.

Ali and Hadji entered the house with Indie on their heels. As usual, the boys tried to play on grandma's love but this time she didn't have any sympathy for them. "You two wanna be like your no-good daddy, huh?" Before they could try to get a word in to sweet-talk her, she said, pointing her fingers in both of their faces, "I don't wanna hear anything you have to say. Every word since you have been here has been a dang-gone lie. I've listened to your foolishness enough, and now you're going to have to listen to me." Ali and Hadji had never seen their grandma like this in their life but they knew it meant that she wasn't playing with them. "Let me tell you two something: Your daddy wasn't anybody whose footsteps you need to be following. He wasn't worth a damn. God forgive me, but these boys have to hear the truth. He wouldn't even want you to follow in his path."

The boys stood in shock, stunned, and didn't utter a word. They had never heard their grandmother speak in this kind of tone to them.

"You running around here disrespecting your momma and this man right here"—Betty pointed to Indie—"and they the only two that ever really gave a damn about you. Khalil wasn't thinking of y'all. I know it hurt to know your daddy ain't worth spit, and it hurt me to have to say that about my own child but the honest to God truth is, he just wasn't."

Hadji was in tears and so was Betty, and hearing herself speak against her son in her own words, she started to break down. "I don't want you to be like your father. Yes, you have many of his traits. In fact, you the spitting image of him, but I want y'all to be the positive version of what he could've been, not the negative version of what he was. I'm looking for y'all to do great things, not just be a mean, evil, bad person like your father was."

The boys couldn't help it, but they cried like they had a chip on their shoulders, wanting to mute Betty out. But Betty couldn't be blocked out; she was on a roll and was too passionate about what she was speaking.

Hadji was angry. He didn't want to hear the awful things his grandmother was saying about his daddy. When he sucked his teeth, Betty hauled off and hit him in the mouth with a swift backhand and then shot him the evil eye.

Before Hadji could get himself together, Betty knew she was losing control. She had never hit either of her grandchildren before in their lives. She walked to her bedroom and got on her knees and prayed. After she finished speaking to her Savior, she got herself together and called them into her bedroom.

Betty hollered down the hall for the boys to come to her room. A moment later they dragged themselves in.

Betty's bed was neatly made with a lot of pillows on it, but her bible rested on the middle of the bed. She was sitting on the edge of the mattress.

"What's up, Grandma?" Betty seemed to have calmed down some but Ali knew that it was best to tread lightly. "Do you need us to run to the store for you or something?" It was rather odd for him to suggest but he didn't know what else to do because he had never saw his grandmother in that state before.

Betty stared at her only two grandbabies. They were already beginning to grow into young men. "Naw, baby, I don't need anything from the store." The boys were watching her with keen eyes as she continued. "I want to talk to you about your father a little more." Her tone wasn't as harsh as it had been just a few minutes ago.

They stood at attention. They could see that her tone was back to the loving grandmother they had known and loved their whole lives. So maybe she would have something positive to say and at least a change of heart toward their father.

She said, "You miss him, don't you?"

It was a simple question, but an honest one. Both Hadji and Ali nodded their heads; they didn't speak. The young had a youthful arrogance that led them to have a tendency to think that older people were senile and forgetful. Maybe they thought if they interrupted her she might forget what she was talking about.

"You don't have to answer because I can see it written all over your faces. You want to be just like him, don't you? That's instinct for a boy: he either wants to be just like his father or nothing like him," she said. "I know I haven't talked too much about my son"—she dropped her head for a second thinking about her words before raising her eyes to meet theirs—"but I had my reasons."

When it came to talking about Lucky, the only person that kept tighter lips than their mother was their grandmother. It was as if the two women had made a convenant with each other to never speak of the man. But the secrecy only helped to fuel the boys' curiosity of who their father really was.

"Khalil didn't have a good heart," Betty bluntly said. "I mean, in his core, I believe his heart was good, but he kept that part of himself hidden from people his entire life. Well, I think in the beginning of your momma and his relationship, she got to see his good side, but other than that nobody else saw it. But he didn't want to hide it from you. He didn't want to conceal his good qualities from you—and you will understand what I mean more after I show you this."

Hadji gazed at his brother, wanting his brother to find the philosopher approach in what their grandmother was saying, but this time Ali didn't know what to make of it, so he just focused all his attention back on his grandmother.

Betty put a DVD in the player that was connected to the forty-two-inch television in front of her bed. After the player took the disc, the screen showed the symbol that indicated the DVD was in the process of being read, and then a picture appeared on the screen.

Lucky was in that picture. The mere sight of him made tears come to the boys' eyes, they were so flustered with emotion.

The twins involuntarily inched closer to the television.

Betty said, "He made this for the two of you before he passed away. I held on to it until I thought you were old enough to really understand what he wanted you to know. I only hope I didn't wait too long." She used the remote to navigate to the part of the disc she wanted them to see and pushed play.

"To my sons, always know that I love you. If you're watching this disc I've long left your lives. This is one of the hardest things I've ever had to do. I don't want either of you to grow up listening to what type of man other people say your father was. I want to be the one to tell you firsthand."

Ali studied the screen intently, every word that came out of his father's mouth.

"I wish I could have done better by you and your mother. Tressa was the best thing that ever happened to me. In return for the love she showed me I gave her nothing but hurt and misery. The best thing that could have happened for you two was when your mother got tired of my bullshit and left me."

Hadji was pissed off because this wasn't what he wanted to hear, but nevertheless he continued to listen attentively.

"Even after she left I still tried to make her life miserable because my ego was so big that I didn't want to believe that she could be better off without me in her life. But she was. There was no doubt, she would probably be dead if she'd stayed. Nothing good could grow in my presence because I wouldn't allow it. I didn't want it."

Lucky kept going as both boys stood mesmerized.

"You may hear a lot of things about me, most of it bad. Because anybody that has anything good to say about me was either scared of me, stupid, or just flat-out lying. And that's the honest truth. But the only thing I regret in this life is not doing right by your mother. She deserved so much better."

Still transfixed by the image and words of their father, the twins broke down and cried. Really hard.

"If you'll allow me to ask one favor of you it'll be this: don't grow up to be like me. I was a piece of shit and am probably rotting in hell for the things that I've done."

When Betty pushed the stop button both twins were still crying. Betty took them into her arms and embraced them.

Ali said, "So Momma was telling the truth after all."

24

Surprise

The boys had been settled back at home for over a month. Things were finally falling in place and Tressa and Indie's big day was approaching. A week before the wedding, thirty of Indie and Tressa's closest friends and family gathered at their home for an intimate yet extravagant luncheon that Missy had happily planned for the happy couple.

"Everything looks so lovely and delicious," Ivy said to Tressa as she admired the seafood spread, which included six different types of shrimp, mini crab cakes, crab, seafood dip, stuffed salmon, and seafood salad. "And who did the veggies and fruit? I just love how the fruit display is done." Ivy leaned in and motioned toward an ice sculpture, a six-feet-tall heart-shaped ice sculpture with the happy couple's initials "T" and "I" that was the focal point of the food table, before taking a sip of her champagne. "It's just perfect for you two lovebirds."

"I wish I could take responsibility for this"—Tressa smiled, admiring the arrangement—"but Missy is responsible for everything." Tressa was proud of what a fantastic and elaborate job her friend had done for her and Indie.

"I think I'm going to have to get Missy to help me put together my next event," Ivy said as she contemplated breaking her diet for a slice of red velvet cake.

Just then the doorbell rang.

Indie saw that Tressa was preoccupied. "I'll get it." And a couple of minutes later, he walked back into the room with a special guest.

Tressa ran across the floor like a little girl to give her brother a hug. Then she hit him. "You are late," she teased as the photographer snapped several pictures of the smiling siblings, who were a mirror reflection of each other.

Taj had an alibi. "I just got to town a few hours ago. The airport was a mess and they gave me hell renting a car."

"Man you know a rental wasn't necessary. We would've let you use one of our cars," Indie said to his brother-in-law-to-be. The two had a bond that no one could come between. They both had an undying love for Tressa and would do anything to keep her safe and happy.

"Besides, I wanted to surprise you," Taj said looking to Tressa. "Surprise."

Tressa introduced Taj to a few of her friends that he didn't already know. After a round of "nice to meet yous" and shaking hands, Taj asked about the his nephews.

"They are upstairs, probably under the spell of one of those video games," Tressa told him. "Go up there and let them know you are here. You know they love themselves some crazy-ass Uncle Taj."

"Runs in the family," Taj quipped. He took off for the steps to check on his nephews before Tressa could come back with something slick to say.

Taj made his way up to the boys' room.

"Uncle Taj!" Ali was the first to spot him when Taj peeked his head through the door.

"No one told us you were coming," Hadji said excitedly.

"You know I wouldn't miss your momma's wedding for all the world and everything in it."

Hadji had his mind wrapped around one thing: "What you bring us?" Ever since the twins were babies they could always count on their Uncle Taj for a spectacular gift whenever he came to visit.

Taj never lied to his nephews (almost never) and he wasn't going to start now. "I left it in the car," he said. "I heard you two been acting a fool so I wasn't sure if I was going to hit y'all off or not."

The twins looked up to their uncle and Taj felt guilty because he knew his sister's sons needed him. He wished he had spent more time with his nephews, and seeing them made him realize that he should've been there more for them, but there was no room for dwelling on the past.

"That's old news. We got our sh-stuff together now," Ali said.

Taj nodded. "I'm glad to hear that because y'all had your mother real stressed out. I thought I was going to have to come and bust some asses up in this joint for a minute." The twins weren't sure if their uncle was kidding or not, and Taj liked it that way.

"For real though, it's all good that you're on the straight and narrow but how about telling me about what you did this summer?" Taj had heard most of the stuff from the grapevine, not to mention what Tressa had told him, but he wanted to give his nephews a chance to come clean. "I want to know what you were really into," he said.

Both boys were quiet, and then Taj asked, "Anything y'all wanna talk about? I know y'all been having a lot on your mind and it's been tough for y'all even though y'all back on the right track. By the way I'm proud of y'all for getting your shit together but like I said, anything you want to talk about?"

The twins looked at each other and over the next forty-five minutes the twins told Taj every detail of their eventful last couple of months. It was Ali who began the confessional, "The dude Ace, who use to be our daddy's friend, kinda played the shit out of us."

"What?" Taj was shocked to hear his nephews going so hard. Then he thought again that it shouldn't really have been a surprise; he knew that the boys had been hanging out with Ace but Indie told him he straightened it out.

"Thought Indie took care of Ace."

"He did," Hadji said, and shot Ali a look that said, "be quiet."

But Ali kept speaking, "It's just that when we was hanging with him, he convinced us to do something that might hurt momma in a way or another."

"What might hurt your momma?"

"Well, if something happened to Indie."

"Ain't nothing going to happen to Indie," Taj said.

"We can't be sure about that because Ace really thinks that Indie killed our daddy and that momma had something to do with it, and now since Indie punked him in front of everybody, he's got to get even."

Hadji jumped in at that moment. "And it was so gangsta

too the way he did it." He got excited. "I always thought that he was soft, but it was like he was somebody else that day."

"Yeah he's thorough," Taj admitted. "There's nothing soft about that dude. Trust me, there's more to him than meets the eye. So don't let the moccasins fool you." He gave both boys a firm look. "That's real."

"Then our friend Tommy heard that Ace took money for a hit that he tried to have us do."

"A hit?"

"Yeah," Ali said that and more, but Taj had heard enough.

Taj left his nephews and mingled around the party for a little while longer but he couldn't get what the boys had told him off his mind. Enough was enough! When nobody was looking, Taj slipped off with one thing on his mind: to go straighten the score with Ace once and for all.

25

Uncertainties

As the party went on, more and more liquor was being consumed, which meant things were getting lively. The Grey Goose had done its job and most of the guests were loose as a goose, dancing and having a great time. Surprisingly, besides Tressa, the only other person who had not been drinking was Hondo. After his last accident, he was done with drinking. Instead he sat in the corner in his wheelchair watching everybody, enjoying himself, living vicariously through his son's happiness—that was intoxicating enough.

The great room had been transformed into a dance floor. All the furniture had been removed, leaving nothing but the glistening hardwood floors. The deejay played the cha-cha slide, and almost all of the guests were participating in the line dance. Ivy loved to dance and she owned the dance floor like it was hers. It was no surprise because dance had always been a major part of her life. In fact, she had won first place in a modern dance competition in college, ironically the same night that Marvin had introduced her to Eli. Now that Ivy thought about it, where was Eli? She had been so preoccupied by the wine and the line dances that she realized she had not seen her husband in quite a few songs. Once the cha-cha slide went off and a slow song came on, she left the dance floor to look for Eli.

Ivy headed to the kitchen, then to the living room, the den, and the library looking for her husband. She even went to the bathroom to see if maybe Eli was indisposed. But as she reached the bathroom and was about to knock, Indie's sister, Reka, came out of it. The more she couldn't find Eli, the more it puzzled her. He was nowhere to be found. *Where in the hell was Eli?*

Frustrated that she couldn't find him downstairs, Ivy decided to look upstairs. Holding a half-full glass of wine in one hand, she used the other to grip the railing to proceed up the stairs to continue her search. When Ivy was halfway up the steps, Tressa looked up and happened to notice her. Tressa thought it was odd and wondered what in the world Ivy could possibly be looking for upstairs in her house, so Tressa followed her.

Ivy made her way from room to room barging in, and when she finally got to one of the guest bathrooms she didn't even bother to knock. She simply pulled the door open. It was often said, when one looks, one won't find, but Ivy got what she was and wasn't looking for. Stunned, Ivy couldn't believe her eyes. She had gotten the shock of her life.

Inside the bathroom, Eli's pants were around his ankles and Marvin was bent over the sink. Eli was putting wood in him something fierce.

"What the *fuck*?" Ivy said, in a slurred, high-pitched tone. She threw her wineglass down and then Hurricane Ivy stormed in behind it. She pushed her way through the bathroom door.

"You disgusting son of a bitch, you! What the hell do you

think you're doing?" she screamed as she grabbed the decorative knickknacks that lay around the powder room, trying to hit them both.

For the first time that Ivy could remember, her husband was speechless.

But she really didn't give him a chance to answer anyway. As Eli tried to pull up his pants, she picked up the metal cover that held a tissue box and hit her husband upside the head. Instead of Marvin getting out of the way, he got on some other stuff. Marvin acted like he wanted to fight Ivy—as if he was defending his man, Eli.

"Get your hands off of him, you ungrateful bitch!"

Ivy paid his jealous rant no mind. Instead she unleashed her fury on Eli. "You bitch-ass motherfucker!" She screamed at the top of her lungs. "I'm going to kill you!"

Ivy started raining blows upside Eli's head. She was like a wild bull in a china shop and seemed to have the strength of Hercules.

Tressa tried to break it up but she couldn't get them apart. "Stop, hold on." She tried to separate them by getting in between Ivy and Marvin. But Eli had turned on his lover, and now was hitting Marvin for hitting Ivy. But there wasn't much that Eli could really do to defend Ivy because his pants were all the way down to his ankles. Everything had happened so fast that he hadn't had a chance to button them up. Besides, Ivy didn't really need the help, because the combination of alcohol and anger that came with finding her husband screwing another man had made her strong as an ox.

"Come on y'all, stop!" Tressa said as she tried to get Marvin out of the way, but he pushed Tressa off of his back, knocking her to the floor. Like a jack-in-the-box, she jumped back up. But before she knew it, her boys were out of their room and in the middle of the mix. The twins were on Marvin now, double banking him. They somehow had gotten him down on the floor and were getting the best of Marvin.

"Help! Help! Indie!" Tressa called out for assistance to get things under control. Only no one from downstairs could hear her over the music.

Ivy now had all her attention focused on Eli and was giving him blows to the head like a skilled professional boxer. Meanwhile, Tressa ordered, "Marvin, leave! Boys, let him up and help me."

Tressa was still in a bit of shock; she had no idea that the person that Eli was having an affair with was right under her nose. And even more surprising: it wasn't another woman after all.

The boys immediately followed her instructions and stopped hitting Marvin, but not before getting one last lick in as Hadji said, "Don't you ever in your life think about putting your hand on my mother again."

Before Ali could begin to try to help his mother get control of the situation, Indie appeared, pulling Ivy off of Eli. "What the fuck is going on in here?" he asked.

And that's when Ivy snapped out of her trance. She released the tight chokehold she had managed to clamp on Eli's neck, and her anger turned into tears. She slid down the bathroom wall like one of those women in a Lifetime movie and began to weep. "Eli, how could you? How could you do this to me? How could you do this to us?"

Tressa didn't know what to do; she felt awful for Ivy.

Eli tried to hug her, and Ivy stopped him in his tracks. "Get the *fuuckkk* away from me!"

Tressa looked at Eli and motioned for Indie to take him to another part of the house quietly. She didn't want the other guests to know about the commotion that had been camouflaged by the music.

Tressa took a deep breath and sat on the floor beside Ivy. Before she spoke, she took Ivy in her arms. "It's going to be okay. I don't know how, but it's going to be okay."

Ivy didn't say a word, she just cried from the depths of her soul. After a few minutes and a lot of tissues, the tears eventually slowed down. Ivy began to apologize. "Tressa, I'm so sorry," she said between sniffles.

"What are you sorry for?" Tressa asked.

Ivy wiped her nose. "Ruining your get-together," she said between sobs.

"No." Tressa shook her head. "You didn't ruin my night. This isn't your fault. You didn't do anything. I'm sorry this happened to you."

When Tressa said those words to Ivy, it was almost like something clicked off in her head, "Did you know?"

Tressa read Ivy's face, and she could see the betrayal not only from Eli but from Tressa too. While Tressa knew that Eli was having an affair, she had no idea that it was with Marvin. Even if she did, it didn't matter because Tressa's poker face was on so tight it could've been botoxed. "God, no. I had no idea that Eli was having an affair with Marvin. I was just as surprised as you were."

Ivy studied Tressa's face to see if she was lying.

When Ivy couldn't find any indication that Tressa was telling her anything but the truth, she just hugged her. "Oh, I'm so sorry about all this, ruining your bathroom and your special night."

"Awww, I'm okay. I'm just glad you didn't kill him in my house with that left hook." Tressa tried to lighten up the mood.

Indie came back upstairs and peeped into the bathroom and saw both women sitting side by side on the floor. He asked, "Is everything okay, babe?"

"Yeah, we're hanging in here, trying to clear our heads from some of this blurry shit."

Ivy stared off into the air. "It's so sad and ironic, how things are."

"What do you mean?" Tressa asked.

"The ending of one marriage happens at the beginning of another."

Those words left Tressa speechless. Taking those words in sent her into deep thought. What would this mean for Eli? The campaign? Her life? Her job? Her livelihood? Her family? Wow, she thought, the moment it seemed as if things were certain, there were so many other uncertainties. The only thing that she was positively sure about was getting married to the love of her life, and at that minute nothing else really mattered.

26

An Ace in a Hole

Swish. The sound of the basketball going through the hoop touching nothing but the net was music to Ace's ears. He tracked the ball down, corralled it, dribbled back out to the three-point arc, edging his Air Jordans up to the line, he pushed off another shot.

Swish. Practice makes perfect.

The sun had risen an hour and half ago, and Ace had been pumping off jumpers for two-thirds of the day's first light. Same way he did every morning ever since waking up in prison long ago. He liked being on the court early and alone. Shooting hoops in solitude gave him the opportunity to get a little needed exercise as well as time to reflect and meditate. These times also reminded him of his high school days.

Swish.

He was pretty good at basketball and had probably been good enough to get a scholarship to play ball if he hadn't got busted for breaking into a house during his sophomore year at Kennedy High. Full speed to the basket, he caught the ball before it could bounce a second time after falling out of the net, and laid it back against the backboard.

"Whew!" He was breathing hard, face shining with perspiration as he tried to catch his second wind, when out of the corner of his eye, he saw an unfamiliar blue Impala bend the edge of the projects. Needles of prickly hair rose on the back of his neck. *Fuck!* A sudden, uncanny sensation of eminent danger tickled his spine. He couldn't explain it, but a person who did others dirty on a regular basis knew trouble when it was coming his way.

The car was moving too slow. Not casually in no hurry, but slow. This was more like creeping slow, scoping slow, hunting slow.

There were at least two people inside. He tried making out a face but because of the distance and glare from the morning sun he was unable to do so. But the "who" wasn't important right now, it was the "what." Ace needed two things: a gun, which he didn't have, and an escape route to get the fuck out of dodge.

One thing he *did* have in his favor was that he knew the projects like he knew his baby momma's coochie. Intimately— inside and out.

Ace dropped the ball and hauled tail. He heard the engine of the Impala revving as he broke around the monkey bars and then across the field around the 4600 apartment building. There were more than five hundred units that made up Cyprus Court. The recreation center was its nucleus. Ace wanted to make it to Murphy Lane, which was roughly four or five blocks away, to 9002, apartment H, and then he'd be home free, because that's where his SK assault rifle was hidden.

He covered three of the blocks without ever setting foot on the street. It was impossible to be followed by a car. All he had to do was get across Berkley Lane to reach Murphy, which was less than two blocks away. He was breathing heavily, mostly from adrenaline, and his familiarity with his surroundings was helping him beat the odds. Looking in both directions, just to be sure, before coming out into the open space, Ace shot across the street with what looked to be a smile of relief stamped on his face.

There was a problem. Ace took one thing for granted. He wasn't the only one familiar with the terrain. Ace hadn't heard the shots until after he felt the hot balls cut through his body. One went in his side and came out of his stomach. The other pierced his right leg. He could feel his flesh searing, but kept it moving as best he could. A bullet that ripped through Ace's gut, taking piece of his kidney with it, then exited, caused the most damage. The one still lodged in his upper right thigh made it impossible for him to run any farther, but he found some bushes to hide in for the time being.

Ace collapsed in the bushes. He rolled near some shrubbery, praying that whoever was in the car didn't come searching, and instead, would consider the job done and keep going. If they came looking to finish the job, Ace knew that he was as good as cooked.

The next few seconds felt like forever. Then he heard the tires of the car peel off. *There must really be a God for gangsters,* he thought. However, his body was too beat up and exhausted to move on its own power, so he laid there and waited to get his strength back before he would move into the open where someone could see him and help him.

Then he heard a noise. Footsteps. Coming in his direction. He thought it was his imagination. He sat still holding his breath. Hoping they would go away, but they didn't. They only got louder and closer.

"Shit!" he said under his breath. Ace cursed the same God he had prayed to and thanked moments before.

He had his eyes squeezed shut, sweat pouring down his face, body wrung out like an old dishrag when he felt his executioner standing above him. This was it. He knew the day would come sooner or later but he always prayed for later. Live by the gun, die by the gun. For some odd reason he thought about Indie, how Indie was wrong about him. "I'm not a coward," he mumbled, and opened his eyes to face his killer, man to man. He felt the chances of them meeting again in hell were better than average and Ace wanted to remember and recognize that man.

"Tommy," he whispered, "I'm glad you're here, lil' bro." He was relieved to see help. He let off a little smile because maybe God had the gangster's back after all.

Tommy had been sitting on his porch and seen Laylo and Dirty Red get the jump on Ace. He pulled out a switchblade identical to the ones that Tressa had taken from Ali and Hadji. The reflection from the sun off the razor-sharp blade shimmied off Tommy's dark skin and cold stare. "This is for what you did to my mother and father."

Tommy was adopted. His biological mother and father were African. And at that second, it dawned on Ace how much the boy had indeed resembled Radda, the man he and Lucky had robbed and killed over thirteen years ago.

As Taj came around the bend to finish Ace off himself, Tommy beat him to the punch. He plunged the six-inch blade into Ace's neck thirteen times. If Ace wasn't dead, he would have probably laughed at the irony.

27

Until Death Do Us Part

The botanical gardens were sixty acres of exotic, imported, and domestic flowers and shrubbery, creating a breathtaking oasis of plant life. It was a beautiful place to visit . . . and the perfect location for a wedding.

Thirty guests were present at the ceremony. It was a gorgeous Sunday afternoon, not too hot or too cold, and the air was filled with a myriad of fragrances from blossoming flowers. Tressa was firm about having an intimate wedding and not some over-the-top three-hundred-guest extravaganza. Whoever coined the saying "the bigger the better," she was convinced, was probably trying to sell something.

Tressa believed a wedding should be in a place that held some type of meaning. That's why she chose the gardens. When she was a little girl her mother used to bring her and Taj here a few times a year to witness the thousands of flowers and plants in various stages of bloom. Taj didn't really care for the trips all that much, but Tressa thought it was the most beautiful thing she'd ever seen. And she knew her mother would have approved her choice.

Pastor Jacobs stood next to Indie on a meticulously orna-
mented veranda, underneath an arch fabricated with more than
five hundred white orchids and calla lilies.

Guests sat comfortably in cushioned fold-up chairs, draped
with white linen drops, eagerly awaiting the bride to make her
grand entrance. The seating was arranged in five rows of six. And
of course Betty was one of the ones chosen to witness the bride
and groom jump the broom. She wouldn't have missed it for
anything short of an exclusive date with Jesus Christ himself. Ivy
sat next to Betty in the front; she wanted to be as far away from
Eli as possible. No way could she have stomached sitting next to
his "don't ask, don't tell" ass for more than ten seconds. It made
her nauseated just looking at him. But she wasn't there for Eli;
she was there to celebrate a new beginning for Tressa and Indie.

Ivy had put Eli out of the house the same night after catching Eli playing hide the sausage up Marvin's butt. It wasn't like
he gave her much of a choice. Eighteen years was more than
enough of her life to waste on a lie. Out of respect, although she
didn't think he deserved it—God knows he hadn't shown her
any—she promised not to file for the divorce until after the up-
coming election. Eli did have the decency to tell Marvin not to
come to the wedding. Marvin took it hard.

Taj sat in the middle row beside Indie's baby sister, Reka,
trying not to attract too much attention. He intended to hook
up with Missy later in the evening after the reception.

Dutchess was in the back, incredibly happy and surprised to
have received an invitation. Nobody really knew why she was
so surprised that she got an invite, after she broke her neck to
kiss Tressa's ass after she finally accepted Dutchess's phone call.
To be honest, Dutchess would've sat on a cactus plant in the

back of a truck to be there. Until she got the nerve to call Tressa last month (after seeing the twins with Ace at the after-hours spot), it had been a decade since they'd spoken. She knew that backstabbing Tressa was one of the cruelest and dumbest things she had ever done. Tressa had been her best friend since elementary school, always keeping it 100 percent from day one. To show her appreciation for all of Tressa's kindness, Dutchess went and fucked her best friend's man. No guy was worth the friendship she threw away, especially not Lucky's no-good ass. Knowing it would be too much asking Tressa to forget about what had happened, Dutchess was content with one day having Tressa's forgiveness. She would have to wait a bit longer though. Some memories died harder than others.

Up-and-coming songstress Fabiola Mayes graced the ceremony with a song. The girl's voice was like a well-tuned musical instrument. One day Fabiola was going to be a superstar. Near the end of Fabiola's harmonic solo, Tressa arrived in a white horse-driven carriage with Ali and Hadji sitting by her side. The twins were stunningly handsome—striking in their uncanny resemblance to their father—wearing custom-fitted Dolce and Gabbana suits. The duo almost stole the show, but it was Tressa's day, and no one was more eye-catching than the bride in her one-of-a-kind couture dress, which hid her growing baby bump perfectly. The dress was strapless with authentic beading individually sewn into the bodice to create a dazzling iridescence matched only by Tressa's smile.

After she was helped down from the carriage, two people from the dress shop scurried up to primp her attire by smoothing out any creases or shifts that may have occurred during the ride. It was perfect.

Hand in hand, the twins led their mother down the orchid-strewn runner, the words "Beginnings Never to End" featured in script. The summer had been so crazy, with the boys acting out, and there were times that Tressa wasn't sure this moment would ever come to fruition. She decided to wait until after the honeymoon to tell Ali and Hadji that they would soon be big brothers.

Indie tried his best to remain poised and distinguished as he watched Tressa and the twins make that walk, but it was impossible to harness the smile that commanded control of his face at the sight of his wife-to-be. The wait was finally over, he thought, and it was well worth it.

Missy took her spot as the maid of honor. "You look beautiful," she whispered. It was the truth. Tressa was a stunning bride; no one could deny her that fact. And she was an even better person, Missy mused.

Pastor Jacobs ceremoniously cleared his throat and the place got quiet enough to hear the hummingbirds' wings slicing through the air as they flew from flower to flower, seemingly trying to get a front-row seat to see the bride. He began, "I've spoken to Brotha Indie and Sista Tressa over the past couple of months in preparation for this wedding and I've come to find that they are two extremely unique people that are very much in love with each other." Nearly all the guests nodded in agreement. Pastor Walker continued. "They're also very careful and deliberate as they've shown by their marathon engagement of eight years." A light round of laughter tickled the air. "I believe we would have fewer divorces if more couples followed their lead."

Joan Conners yelled out from the fourth row, "Preach,

Pastor!" She was an older white lady that had befriended Tressa when she decided to break out of the mental prison in which Lucky had held her captive.

Ivy felt like the pastor was speaking directly to her. She looked over at Eli in disgust and under her breath, called him a bastard, among a few other choice words.

Taj wondered if he would ever find his ride-or-die bitch. Probably not, he surmised. There weren't many good women to go around, and even fewer good men. Indie and Tressa were blessed to have found each other.

"If anyone here knows of any reason why these two people shouldn't be married today, please stand now or forever hold your peace . . ."

There were a few wry smiles. If anyone did have a beef, no one dared to voice it out loud.

Pastor Jacobs nodded in approval. "Then let us continue."

Brradt! Brradt! Brradt!

The guests incorrectly thought the sudden, rapid succession of explosions were fireworks, an elaborate part of the proceedings. Once they realized that it wasn't staged, and real gunshots had pierced the tranquil moment, pandemonium erupted. The panicked guests started to run for cover.

Taj recognized the distinct sounds of gunfire the moment he heard it. Leaping from his chair with his .40 caliber already drawn, he tried to pinpoint exactly where the shots had originated before the first of the three barrages of gunfire ended. Attempting to avoid the stampede of frightened people coupled with the abundance of places the shooter could hide made the task difficult. There were just too many damn bushes. That was one of the reasons he never liked this place.

Brrradt! Brrradt!

Missy stood in shock, the twins hit the floor, probably wishing they still had the guns Ace had given them as Pastor Jacobs dove off the veranda, an overgrown patch of purple geraniums breaking his fall.

Indie whipped out a nickel-plated sixteen-shot 9mm from the shoulder holster underneath his designer tuxedo jacket. He was glad he'd let Taj convince him to stay packed. "Better safe than sorry," Taj had said, especially after hearing that Indie had punked Ace in front of the entire Cyprus Court. Indie grabbed Tressa by the arm, pulling her down. "Stay down, baby." He used his body to shield hers while searching for the disrespectful fools that had the balls to disrupt his nuptials and put his entire family and the life of his unborn child in harm's way.

Tressa screamed out loud, "My babies!" She was watching the twins, making sure they were okay, but her left arm covered her stomach, her unborn child. *This can't be happening,* she thought as she prayed for God to get her and her family through this situation unharmed. Debris from the orchid archway rained down over their heads like petals of snow.

Indie thought he saw someone peeking from behind a two-story-high Chinese rose bush. Right or wrong, he bucked off a couple of shots in that direction.

Plow! Plow!

All he hit were plants. Rose petals exploded into crimson plumes of smoke.

Taj had a better angle. He followed Indie's shot line with his eyes and caught a glimpse of two faces. It looked like Laylo and Dirty Red.

Apparently they weren't satisfied with just smoking Ace.

Laylo wanted everyone who was responsible for his cousins' deaths. That meant he was after Hadji and Ali, and Laylo didn't give a fuck about collateral damage. Anybody could get it. It didn't matter to him that if he hadn't got upset about losing money fair and square at a craps game and hadn't sent Johnny and Vince on the failed mission to peel Ace's wig and take the loot back that his cousins would still be alive.

"You always were a stupid fuck," Taj mumbled to himself. "And now you went and fucked with the wrong motherfucker's people." Laylo and Dirty Red's reckless abandon had given Taj a clear bead on them both.

Brrradt! Brrradt!

They were shooting wild. It was amazing that no one had been hit yet, Taj thought. Not that he knew of anyway. Let's keep it that way, he thought. Taj was a crack shot.

He took aim, lining Laylo's head up with his sights first and then double tapped the trigger.

Laylo's dome popped.

One down, one to go.

Again, Taj aimed his pistol and took the next shot. He breathed a sigh of relief when he saw he had hit his intended target.

Just as he let his guard down, gunshots came roaring again, and this time no one knew where they were coming from.

The sirens blaring in the background were getting closer. By the time the police arrived, the gunshots had stopped completely. However, no one moved until the police officers began to tell folks everything was okay.

Taj searched for his sister, and finally his eyes met hers. Tressa's heart was racing and tears were rolling down her face.

She held her stomach, her baby, her sons, her brother, and the love of her life. Everything was at stake. It seemed like her life was flashing in front of her eyes. She wished it was a bad dream. Taj could see fear written all over his sister's face; it looked as if she had seen a ghost.

Before staring off into space over her brother's shoulder, Tressa fainted, but not before she said one word:

"Lucky."

A Project Chick

Book 1 in the Project Chick series

available in eBook for the 1st time through

Three Legends Press

A NIKKI TURNER ORIGINAL